"All done," said  **Daddy."**

Philip walked the few feet through the snow and held out his hand for Mary. He turned toward Tasha. "Are you finished, too?"

She nodded, and he held out his other hand to her.

"The secret," said Mary, using the tone of a teacher instructing a class, "is to not get your foot or handprints on the angels. That makes them turn out nice."

"Good advice, Mary," Tasha said as Philip wrapped his hand around hers.

"Heave ho." Philip pulled the girl and the woman up in a single motion. Tasha stood on her feet, her face very close to Philip's. Her lips turned up into a smile. He felt an electric charge that shot down to his toes.

"Thanks for the help," whispered Tasha. Stepping back, she pounded her gloves together to get the snow off them.

Mary jumped up and down clapping her hands. "The angels are perfect, just perfect."

SHARON DUNN

grew up in the country with four sisters and a brother. She loves being out in nature and enjoying God's creation. She lives with her three nearly grown children, her husband of twenty-six years and a very nervous border collie named Bart who often sits at her feet when she writes. You can read more about Sharon and her books at www.sharondunnbooks.net.

SHARON DUNN

Tasha's Christmas Wish

HEARTSONG
PRESENTS

Recycling programs
for this product may
not exist in your area.

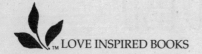
LOVE INSPIRED BOOKS

ISBN-13: 978-0-373-48730-1

Tasha's Christmas Wish

Copyright © 2014 by Sharon Dunn

All rights reserved. Except for use in any review, the reproduction
or utilization of this work in whole or in part in any form by any
electronic, mechanical or other means, now known or hereinafter
invented, including xerography, photocopying and recording, or in
any information storage or retrieval system, is forbidden without
the written permission of the editorial office, Love Inspired Books,
233 Broadway, New York, NY 10279 U.S.A.

This is a work of fiction. Names, characters, places and incidents are
either the product of the author's imagination or are used fictitiously, and
any resemblance to actual persons, living or dead, business establishments,
events or locales is entirely coincidental.

This edition published by arrangement with Love Inspired Books.

® and TM are trademarks of Love Inspired Books, used under license.
Trademarks indicated with ® are registered in the United States Patent
and Trademark Office, the Canadian Intellectual Property Office and in
other countries.

www.Harlequin.com

Printed in U.S.A.

He heals the brokenhearted and binds up their wounds.
—*Psalms* 147:3

For my mother,
who got me started on the love of doll collecting

Chapter 1

From her craft booth, Tasha Henderson watched as a little girl dressed in a red wool coat clutched a stuffed cat and turned in tiny circles, searching the face of each adult who passed by. The child couldn't have been more than six years old. Tasha felt a tightening in her chest. She waited for a mother or father to appear out of the throng of people crammed into the ballroom of the Four Winds Hotel for the Christmas Craft Fair.

Forehead wrinkled and eyes round with fear, the child transferred the stuffed cat from one hand to the other and finally held it close to her chest. From twenty feet away, Tasha couldn't hear the little girl over the mumbling roar of holiday shoppers, but she could see the child mouth the word *Daddy* as she turned in circles.

Pushing through the crowd, Tasha made her way to

the child and touched her arm lightly. "Are you lost, honey?"

"I can't find my daddy." Tears brimmed in big brown eyes. "I wasn't supposed to wander off—" a single tear rolled down her cheek "—but I saw pretty barrettes for my hair." She gulped in air and wiped the tear away with a tight fist.

The little girl's vulnerability touched Tasha. "Why don't you come over here where I'm working?" She pointed to a craft booth that displayed hundreds of porcelain and cloth dolls.

The little girl bit her lower lip and shook her head. "I'm not supposed to go with strangers."

"You're a smart girl." Tasha tapped her fingers on her mouth and glanced back at her booth. "I can't just leave you here. Why don't you tell me your name?"

"Mary." She stroked her stuffed cat's head.

"I promise that you can stay where you can see everybody, and you can look for your father. Is your mother here, too?" Tasha bent slightly so she could make eye contact with Mary.

"My mommy is in heaven with Jesus." The child's voice quivered. She stared at her white boots.

A sting of pain shot straight to Tasha's heart. Were the tears brimming in those deep brown eyes for the temporary loss of her father…or the permanent loss of her mother? Tasha knelt so she could look in her eyes.

Letting go of Mary's arm, Tasha sat back on her heels. Her throat tightened. The child had the same fragility as one of her porcelain dolls. "So how about it? You come back over there with me, and I'll see if there's a loudspeaker in this place, so we can call for your daddy?"

Mary crossed her arms and glanced up at all the people swirling around her. Her forehead wrinkled.

Tasha sweetened the offer. "You can see my dolls." She craned her neck to look over her shoulder at the display booth, three walls of six-foot-tall shelves crammed with dolls. A lower display counter with more dolls completed the fourth side of the booth.

Mary exhaled, her mouth forming an O shape. "Can I hold one?"

"Sure." Something about Mary's wrinkled forehead and furrowed eyebrows—her tendency to think deeply about everything before speaking—reminded Tasha of herself as a child. "You can sit in that chair, so you can still see out on the floor and look for your father, and he can see you if he looks this way."

Wringing her hands, Mary studied the display booth again. "I guess that would be okay."

Tasha held out a hand and tilted her head toward the booth. The child met Tasha's gaze, but shook her head at holding hands. Mary still didn't completely trust her. That was okay. Mary's savvy about dealing with strangers spoke well of how her parents had raised her. "This way." Tasha walked back to the booth, glancing behind her to make sure Mary followed. With the stuffed cat flopped over her shoulder, Mary trudged across the polished floor of the ballroom.

Tasha swept her hand around the doll display. "Now, which one do you want to hold?"

Scanning the shelves, Mary looked at each doll. She set her stuffed cat on the chair. Again, she bit her lower lip, her eyes moving from doll to doll. "That one." She pointed to the sixteen-inch Victorian mother holding a bundled infant in her arms.

"That's one of my favorites." Standing on tiptoe, Tasha grabbed the porcelain lady around the waist. She smoothed out the doll's beige skirt.

Tasha placed the doll in Mary's arms, which she held out in front of her like a cradle. Mary stared down at the milky face with the touch of pink painted on her cheeks; the corners of Mary's mouth turned up slightly. "What's her name?"

"Charlotte."

Mary's eyes brightened. "I have a friend named Charlotte." She adjusted the doll to rest in the crook of her elbow and held a tentative hand above the doll.

"You can touch her if you want," Tasha coaxed.

Mary drew her eyebrows together in an "are you sure?" look, and Tasha gave her a reassuring nod. The child's tiny fingers stroked the mother's face and the sleeping infant. Mary smiled. "You're a nice lady." As she swayed back and forth with the doll, Mary's shoulders relaxed. The lines in her forehead smoothed out.

That was why Tasha liked dolls. Sometimes they could cross barriers of trust that people couldn't. "Now, I'm going to go find out where the intercom is. What is your father's name?"

Mary grabbed Tasha's pant leg. "No, please don't go." The look in the child's eyes was desperate, pleading. Poor dear. Having found someone she could trust, she was probably afraid of being alone again in the crowd.

Tasha glanced around. The booth next to hers was occupied by a woman and her husband who carved large bears and other wildlife out of wood.

"See that lady over there?" Tasha pointed. "I'm going to go and tell her to make an announcement for your father to come to my booth." She touched Mary's slender arm. "I'll stay right here with you. What is your father's name?"

"Philip Strathorn. My aunt is here, too. Her name is Grace, Aunt Grace."

Philip Strathorn? The name sounded familiar. "Why don't you come with me and we'll go tell Linda to broadcast over the loudspeaker?"

Mary held the doll in her bent arm and grabbed Tasha's hand. The tiny cool hand felt light as air in Tasha's. As they walked, Mary glanced down at the doll in her arms and then smiled up at Tasha.

They gave Linda the information. Linda, a petite woman with silver hair in a Betty Crocker style, trotted across the ballroom floor toward the office. In a few minutes, a raspy voice came over the loudspeaker, announcing that Philip Strathorn could find his daughter at Booth 9 on the east side of the ballroom.

Tasha offered Mary a chair while they waited. Several people came by and looked at her dolls. So far, she'd sold just enough dolls to pay for her booth rental, staying in the hotel and the cost of driving to Denver. Tasha's stomach growled. This Christmas craft show was supposed to be her big moneymaker. Breaking even wasn't going to feed her through the winter, let alone buy supplies to make more dolls. Tasha sighed. Nobody ever said starting a business was easy.

Mary rocked back and forth in the chair and held the doll close to her chest, talking sweetly to the Victorian mother and infant. Tasha shook her head as her heart welled up with sorrow. Such a young child without a mother.

"This is a clever idea." A husky female voice caused Tasha to turn her attention back to the booth.

"Cecily Newburg." Tasha exhaled. This was the last place she'd expected to see her former employer. Cecily owned an up-and-coming Denver clothing design firm that catered to the Vail and Aspen crowd.

"Very clever." Cecily tapped a long hot pink fingernail beside the display of custom-made dolls on the counter. Tasha had written a calligraphy sign that said How About a Doll That Looks Like Your Favorite Person? Each doll had a photograph of a real person beside it that Tasha had worked from to create the doll.

"What brings you to the craft show? This is hardly your thing," said Tasha.

"Always looking for new talent, dear, or—" she eyeballed Tasha up and down "—old talent, as the case may be." She tilted her chin up. A cranberry-colored cape that Tasha recognized as one of her own designs was draped over Cecily's tailored suit. She glanced at Mary sitting in the chair. "Don't tell me you're babysitting to earn extra money?"

Cecily Newburg's words stung. Tasha exhaled and lifted her chin. "I'm doing just fine." Despite a growling stomach.

Newburg touched the simple cotton dress of one of the dolls. "If you ever change your mind, you might want to think about moving back to Denver and designing clothes that are a little larger, like for people." Tasha knew that, in actuality, Newburg had short, frizzy blond hair. But today her hair was slicked back off her face and a ponytail extension that fell below her waist perched on top of her head. Rail thin and nearly six feet tall, the clothing designer had a hairstyle that made her look like a genie on steroids.

"Thanks for the offer, but I'm very happy." *Uncertain about the future of my business or where I'll find money for lunch, but happy.*

Cecily Newburg sighed deeply. "Quinton came with me to scout out new talent." Newburg raised her penciled-in, half-circle eyebrows, waiting for Tasha to react. Tasha felt a twitch in her lip, but maintained a neutral face. "I'll send him over to say hello to you if you'd like."

"Thanks, that would be nice." The mention of Quinton stirred her up, and Newburg knew it. Quinton had put so much time into his job as Newburg Design's PR man that he hadn't had much left for Tasha. When she'd moved a long day's drive out of the city back to Montana to start her business and be closer to her mother, it had seemed like a good time to end what was left of the sparse relationship.

"You'll have to stop by the office before you leave." Newburg tapped her long fingernails on the counter. "Get the rest of your stuff as long as you are in town."

Tasha grabbed a strand of her hair and twisted it around her finger. Newburg's piercing gaze unnerved her. "I'm checking out early Monday. I can come by after that if I have time." Why did returning to her former place of employment make her anxious? Was it that it reminded her of all she had given up to pursue this dream? Tasha busied herself straightening a sixteen-inch flapper doll in its stand.

"When you come by," Newburg said, "I might have a surprise for you."

"Really. What?" Tasha's mind raced with the possibilities. Maybe Newburg was going to donate some fabric for her to make doll clothes from. Cecily Newburg had been very clear that she was not happy with Tasha leaving. Still, Tasha kept hoping for a turnaround from Newburg, that she would give some small sign of support for her new venture.

"If I tell, it won't be a surprise, will it?" Cecily grabbed one of Tasha's business cards with her new address and phone number. "You were my best designer, Tasha." She swung around and took a few steps, high heels tapping on the floor. Stopping, she turned her head so Tasha saw her profile. The ponytail looked like a plant sprouting out of her head. "It's a shame to waste your talent on this silliness."

Tasha's jaw muscles tensed, but she held her tongue. Newburg strutted away and was swallowed up by the crowd. Only that obnoxious, artificial ponytail was visible. Tasha felt a lump in her throat the size of a golf ball as she watched the blond hairpiece get smaller and smaller. One by one, she glanced at the serene faces of her dolls. This was not silliness. Tasha gritted her teeth, unable to let go of how Newburg's words had stirred her up.

Tasha looked out on the crowded floor, searching for Mary's father. What would he look like? A worried man racing toward Booth 9, of course.

Philip Strathorn looked for Mary's red coat as he headed toward Booth 9. He'd had only a moment of inattention and Mary had disappeared as they were walking through the ballroom. The fear he'd felt when he turned and couldn't find her had nearly consumed him. It didn't take a psychologist to recognize that even losing Mary temporarily connected back to the loss he felt over his wife's death.

He spotted his daughter sitting in a rocking chair holding a doll. A pretty auburn-haired woman knelt beside her.

"Mary?" His voice chimed above the mumble of the crowd as his spirits lifted.

Mary looked up. "Daddy! Daddy!" Still holding the doll, Mary jumped up from the chair and raced across the floor. He embraced her tightly. "Oh, sweetie, are you okay? I was so worried."

After a long hug, Mary turned to look at the woman. "I was okay. This nice lady helped me."

Philip glanced up at her. "Thank you so much for looking out for Mary." He rose to his feet and held his hand out, and she shook it. "I appreciate your kindness." Her hand was like silk in his. The brief touch sent a surge of warmth up his arm.

"It was the least I could do, Mr. Strathorn." Light came into her eyes. "You're not *Doctor* Strathorn, by any chance?"

"That's me." Philip touched Mary's curly head.

"I thought the name sounded familiar. I've heard you speak at prolife rallies."

Philip smiled. "That's good to hear." He met her gaze momentarily. Her eyes were a soft shade of brown. "It's something I really believe in. I wish I had time to do more of it."

She took a step closer to Philip. "You were inspiring when you did speak."

Mary tugged on her father's shirt. "She makes pretty dolls. Can we get one, Daddy? Can we, huh?" Mary placed the mother doll in Philip's hands.

His finger touched the bundled infant in the mother's arms. A wave of grief hit him. It had been over a year since Heather's death. He just never knew when the sadness would spring up and catch him off guard.

"Very beautiful," he whispered. Regaining his composure, he studied the other dolls. His eyes rested on the custom-made doll display. "Very impressive. The resemblance between the photo and the doll is remarkable."

"Thank you." She glowed from the compliment.

"Can we get one, Daddy?" Mary held her hands together and bounced. "Please."

"Right now, we need to go meet Aunt Grace and your cousins for lunch. Daddy will think about it." He handed the mother doll back to the woman. "I can't thank you enough for helping Mary. I didn't catch your name."

"Tasha. Tasha Henderson."

He scooped his daughter up. "I don't know what I'd do without my little princess." Mary laughed and pressed her forehead against his. "Thank you again."

Mary wrapped her arms around her father's neck and rested her head on his shoulder. The child's touch was like butterfly wings and sunshine all rolled together. He was so glad he had her in his life.

He glanced over his shoulder at the woman as she straightened her dolls and an idea sparked in his head.

Chapter 2

By late afternoon, Tasha had sold several more dolls, but had taken no orders for the custom-made dolls. She decided that rather than spend the money on an expensive hotel dinner, she would just stay in her hotel room and eat the granola bars and fruit she'd brought with her from home.

As the crowd thinned, she noticed Quinton talking to a woman who sold clothing that looked like it included elements of tie-dye and quilting. Quinton was dressed in his long wool coat. She didn't need to get closer to him to know that his trousers would have no wrinkles and his shoes would look as though they'd just come out of the box. The young woman threw back her head and laughed at something Quinton said as he ran his fingers through his wavy blond hair.

"I'd like to get this doll for my granddaughter."

Tasha drew her attention back to a silver-haired woman holding the Shirley Temple–like doll in the red polka-dot dress. The woman clicked her purse open.

Tasha nodded. She touched the doll's ringlets. "I'm sure your granddaughter will love it." She poured so much time and love into each doll that when she did sell one, she felt like a teacher saying goodbye to a graduating student.

The woman placed a credit card on the counter. "Meagan likes dolls, even at her age."

Tasha wrapped the doll in tissue paper. "How old is your granddaughter?"

"Meagan's seventeen. She's going off to college this fall. I thought the doll would be a nice reminder of home. She can have it in her dorm room to remind her of how much her Grammy loves her."

Tasha placed the doll in a box. "Dolls are a good way to remember someone special."

"This doll looks like my little Meagan when she was starting off to school, just six years old." The woman sighed deeply. "The time goes by so quickly."

"That's what my mom always said." Tasha placed the cover on the box and handed it to the woman. "I hope Meagan likes her gift."

As the older woman walked away with her treasure, Tasha glanced at the booth where Quinton had been. He was gone.

She shook off the rising tension she felt in her neck and shoulders. Quinton and Newburg were her old life. She looked around at the myriad dolls—some smiling, some sad, some old, some young. *This*—she rested her gaze on the blue eyes of a lady doll in a flowing purple ball gown—*is my new life.* She glanced at several other dolls. *And these are my new coworkers.* She smiled. *They're not a bad crowd to work with.*

She stopped for a moment when she got to the doll depicting an older woman sitting in a chair with her needlework. The doll's head tilted to the side and her gray-and-white hair was pulled up into a loose bun. "Hello there, Mama." Tasha had painted a clear glaze over the hazel eyes to mirror the glittering brightness of her own mother's eyes.

Tasha had been an only child and a late-in-life baby. Her father, a gentle man with a weak heart, had died when she was five. Maybe that was why she was so sympathetic to Mary's loss. Her mother and, as Tasha put it, a hundred other moms and dads at church had raised her. Moving back to Montana wasn't just about starting the business. Her mom's failing health had clinched the deal. She'd be home soon enough to hug the real "mama."

Tasha noticed Mary's stuffed cat and picked it up. The image of Philip holding Mary flitted through her mind. She'd felt a little spark when Philip had looked over his shoulder at her. Just a chance encounter—she'd probably never see the two of them again. Maybe she could leave the cat at the front desk and hope they'd come looking for it.

She slumped down in her chair and stared out at the thinning crowd. Closing time was only a few minutes away.

The wind kicked up and the temperature dropped as Philip opened the trunk of his car and pulled his briefcase out. Already, biting needles of snow stung his skin. Shading his forehead with his hand, he looked up at gusting snow and dark sky. This storm was going to be a doozy. He slammed the trunk shut.

Once inside the lobby of the hotel, he rested the briefcase on a chair and clicked it open. He unzipped an inside pocket and pulled out a five-by-seven photograph. Each time he removed the photograph, he told himself he wouldn't look at it. He told himself that keeping the picture of his wife and daughter close by was a way of getting through the grief, but looking at it was torture.

Each time he told himself that, and every time he ended up staring at the photograph of the smiling woman with dark brown hair and gray-green eyes and the beautiful child she held in her arms. The sharp pain of loss had subsided into the intense ache of grief. He wondered if that ache, that longing to come home and find his wife and daughter making cookies and laughing, would ever go away.

This time, though, he was going to do something positive, something healing with this photograph, for Mary anyway. An idea had germinated when he'd seen Mary holding the Victorian doll with the bundled-up baby.

He'd dropped Mary off with her cousins and aunt so he could talk to Tasha Henderson about his idea without Mary knowing.

He strode toward the ballroom. When he arrived, the doors to the ballroom were still open, but only a few people milled around. Most of the booths were covered with sheets.

A security guard strode toward him. "Can I help you, sir? This place if going to be closing up in about two minutes."

Disappointment settled in, making his shoulders slump. "I was looking for the woman in Booth 9." He pointed in the general direction. "The pretty redhead with all the dolls."

"Oh, yeah. I know the one," said the security guard. "She left less then a minute ago. Said something about going upstairs to her room. You might be able to catch her."

Philip patted the security guard's shoulder. "Thanks." He ran toward the stairs, hoping he wasn't too late. As he hurried, he realized that this wasn't just about getting a doll made for Mary. He was glad to have an excuse to talk to Tasha again.

As she made her way through the lobby, people sauntered through the hallways with room key cards in their hands. The hotel was packed.

Her room was on the fifth floor, but a meal of granola bars and tea was nothing to race up the stairs for. She stopped in the hallway and kicked off her shoes. Leaning against the wall, she rubbed her calf with her bare foot. Standing all day was hard on her legs. She put her shoes back on and thought about finding a deli or someplace that served cheaper meals than the hotel offered. But the snowstorm beating against the tall glass windows told her that was not a good idea.

She walked the long hallway to the stairs, passing groups of people. Holding the stuffed cat, she trudged up the stairs. She hesitated. She'd intended to leave the cat at the front desk. Her calves ached and her back muscles bunched up like strands of knotted rope. She could take the stuffed cat down after a meal and a hot bath when she felt refreshed. She massaged a sore spot on her shoulder. Right now, she didn't feel like dealing with anything. She was on her second flight of stairs when she heard pounding footsteps behind her.

Someone called her name.

Tasha glanced down the stairs.

When she turned around, several people stepped by her on the stairs offering only a passing glance. Then Philip Strathorn rushed around the corner and stopped on the landing. "Tasha Henderson."

"Yes." Tasha walked down several steps to the landing. He stood close enough for her to smell the woody scent of his cologne. He bent his head down. His hair was the same light brown as Mary's, but not curly.

"I asked the security guard if he'd seen the pretty redhead from Booth 9." Philip leaned against the wall. "He said you'd gone this way. I couldn't talk to you earlier because I had Mary with me."

Heat rose up in Tasha's cheeks. So that was the impression she'd given him, that she was pretty.

Philip continued, "I know this is rude of me. I should have caught you before you closed down shop for the day."

"No, it's all right." Tasha liked the gentleness she saw in Philip's brown eyes. She tucked a strand of hair behind her ear. "I don't mind."

"I need you to create two custom-made dolls for me." Taking his hand away from the wall, he stood up straight, waiting for her response.

"Two dolls?" Tasha's tired feet felt a little less sore. Fatigue melted off her neck and shoulder muscles. Two custom dolls would cover the cost of heat and electric for her studio, enough supplies for maybe ten more dolls and dinner at the café with Mom. "Those dolls are labor intensive. The price would be close to a thousand dollars for two dolls."

"Price is no object." Philip pulled a photograph from the inside pocket of his ski jacket. He handed her the picture, his eyes searching. "It's my wife, Heather, with Mary."

Tasha stared down at two bright faces: a woman holding a little girl in her arms. Now she knew where Mary got her curly hair. They were dressed in matching red sweaters. The woman's coloring was darker than Mary's, but she had the same heart-shaped face. Soft gold lights twinkled in the background.

"Heather died over a year ago. I thought maybe if Mary had a doll to hold—" Philip shifted his weight from one foot to the other.

His expression darkened, which had the same effect on his face as a cloud passing over the sun. She noticed the slight glazing of his eyes, that almost indiscernible sadness. Guilt washed over her. This man and his daughter were hurting. How dare she think of the dolls only in terms of monetary gain?

He sighed deeply. "Maybe this is a dumb idea." He held out his hand for the photograph.

"It's not a dumb idea at all." She drew the photograph closer to her chest and looked him in the eye. "Dolls give children comfort and maybe healing, too." With the stuffed cat flung over her shoulder, she touched his arm. "You know, when abused children are brought to shelters, one of the first things they give them is a teddy bear or a doll. It makes them feel safe. When a child has to go to a new place, a hospital or something, holding a doll comforts them. It's not a dumb idea, Dr. Strathorn." The emotion in her words surprised her. Was she trying to convince herself as well as Philip that doll making wasn't *silliness?*

"Thank you, I needed to hear that." His shoulders relaxed. The corners of his mouth turned up slightly. "Please, call me Philip."

She still held his arm just above the elbow. She let go of him and drew her attention back to the photo. She hadn't intended to speak so passionately.

He touched the photo she held in her hand. "Mary cries every night. Sometimes she has bad dreams. I thought maybe the doll would do what I can't—make her feel as if her mother is near." He shrugged. "I don't know. It might comfort her."

A lump formed in her throat. "I think it's a beautiful idea, Philip." He had worry lines on his forehead, much too prominent for a man who was probably not past thirty-five. He smiled faintly, but she saw the tightness in his jaw. "My order forms are back at the booth. Are you going to be around tomorrow?" She pulled one of her cards out of her purse and placed it in his hand.

"My sister has a room here. I was going to go back to the house with Mary, but I don't want to drive in this storm. Mary can spend more time with her cousins this way anyhow."

"You live here in Denver?" Tasha shifted the stuffed cat to the crook of her elbow.

"Yes, how about you?"

"I used to. I moved back to my hometown, Pony Junction." Still wrestling with the stuffed cat, she placed the photo inside the purse and snapped it shut. "I don't suppose you've heard of it. It's a little town in Montana. It was cheaper to start a business there, and I'm closer to my mom."

"Actually, I have heard of it. It's about thirty miles from where my sister and her family live in Monroe Springs. Mary and I spend time there when I can get away from my practice, which isn't often."

Philip pulled a business card out of his wallet. "This is my office number. If you need to discuss the project, it would be best if you didn't call me at home. I don't want to spoil the surprise for Mary."

She shifted the stuffed cat again so she could take the card from Philip.

Smiling, Philip lifted the toy out of her arms. "I can take this off your hands."

"Sorry, I'd grown so used to having him, I'd forgotten that he wasn't mine." They both laughed. "So I'll see you tomorrow." She turned to go up the stairs.

"Listen—" He hesitated. "Since I bothered you after you were officially closed, why don't I make it up to you? I'll buy you dinner—that is, of course, if you don't mind eating with my sister's kids and Mary."

Tasha turned back around. Philip seemed nice enough, but she hardly knew him.

Philip held up the stuffed cat. "You could personally return Mr. Happy. My daughter would think you were a hero."

Tasha stared down at the plastic eyes of the cat. "Is that his name?" Her growling stomach made up her mind for her. "A nice meal sounds wonderful. I'd be glad to join you."

"Good, I'm supposed to meet Grace and the kids downstairs in about ten minutes." He flopped the stuffed cat over one arm like a coat.

"Lead the way," said Tasha.

Chapter 3

Philip heard the chatter of voices and the tinkle of plates and silverware before they stepped through the big French doors of the Four Winds restaurant. The pungent aroma of rosemary and fresh hot bread greeted him. Almost every table was occupied.

The dining room featured a high ceiling with three crystal chandeliers. On the far wall, diners sat beneath a painted panorama of a forest beside a lake with white-capped mountains towering in the background. At each corner of the mural, a cherublike creature blew wind from his puffed cheeks.

Philip requested a table in the middle of the room so Grace and the kids would be able to see them. Tasha sat down opposite him and opened her menu. The light played across her face, giving her a warm glow. She was very pretty in an unassuming way.

His sister and the kids appeared at the entryway. "Grace, over here." Philip waved.

Grace stopped a few feet short of the table and stared at Tasha. "Philip, I had no idea you could buy people at the craft fair." Grace was a stout, broad-shouldered woman with short, wavy brown hair and a smile that took up most of her face. She was dressed simply but elegantly in black slacks, a print silk tank top and a matching big shirt.

Philip laughed. "This is Tasha. She's going to help me with the secret."

"Oh, right, the secret," said Grace as she took a seat to the left of Philip.

"What secret, Daddy?" Mary sat in the chair beside him. The pastel pink of her dress made her skin seem even paler. A lace collar paralleled the curve of her chin and jaw.

"If I tell you, it won't be a secret anymore." Philip put his head close to hers so their noses touched.

"Please, Daddy." She pulled back and wrinkled her nose at him, a look that never ceased to delight him.

"No, princess, I'm not telling." Philip held her chin in his hand.

His niece and older nephew slipped into their chairs while their little brother crawled onto his mother's lap. Sucking two fingers, he rested his head against Grace's chest.

Philip tousled the older boy's hair. "These are my nephews, Travis—" the boy smiled, revealing braces "—and Shawn." Shawn turned his head and snuggled into his mother's shirt. Grace touched his fuzzy head.

His niece piped up, "And I'm Damaris." Two blond

braids fastened with round bobbles framed Damaris's face. She wore a hot pink sweater with a bunny on it.

Tasha nodded at each of the children.

"Tasha just moved to Pony Junction." Philip lifted his glass of ice water.

"Really, whereabouts do you live?" Grace unrolled Travis's napkin and placed it across his lap.

"I renovated the old barn on Gurston Road."

"I know where that is. We're just about thirty miles from there. The organic food farm, just off Weaver."

"I've seen the signs. There are a lot of little one-horse towns all around that area," said Tasha.

"My husband, Gary, drives a truck during the winter to help make ends meet. Things are tight sometimes, but I really like living in the country." Grace took a sip of water and gazed at Philip over the top of her glass. "I keep trying to talk Philip into moving. We could use a good doctor out there, and Mary would get to see her cousins more."

"Grace, don't get started. You know my practice is established here in Denver." Philip raised his eyebrows at his sister. "I have no desire for small-town life."

Grace unfolded her napkin. "He never would listen to his older sister," she teased.

The waiter came by and they ordered. While they waited for their meals to arrive, the conversation turned to what they had seen at the craft show. Everyone chattered as steaming plates of food were set in front of them. Philip inhaled the citrus scent of his roast duck. His mouth watered as they bowed their heads to say grace.

Tasha whispered, "Amen," and lifted her head. With a glance at her, he silently thanked God for the blessing of a good meal and company before scooping up a forkful of mashed potatoes and gravy.

"Can we go to the pool after dinner?" Travis shoved a French fry slathered with ketchup into his mouth.

"I don't see why not," Grace said. She turned to Tasha. "We'd love to have you join us if you don't have any plans after dinner." Grace offered Philip a raised-eyebrow look that he recognized.

Grace must have seen how he stared at Tasha and decided to play matchmaker. He'd flirted with the idea. She seemed nice, but they lived in different cities and had very different lives.

"Just television and an early night. I have to get up at six to open the booth. I don't have a swimsuit with me, but you guys would certainly be better company than the nightly news."

"It's settled, then," said Grace. "Come join us at the pool."

The children took the lead in the conversation, chatting about school, pets and what they wanted for Christmas.

While they ate, Philip snuck a glimpse at Tasha as she joked with Damaris about some new toy he'd never heard of. She was a natural around children. Yes, she was pretty and very kind. Still, he found himself making excuses for keeping their relationship strictly business. He wasn't ready for anything else just yet.

After dinner, Tasha went upstairs to freshen up before meeting the others at the pool. During the meal, Tasha had sensed that Philip was staring at her, but when she glanced in his direction he looked at his plate.

Was there more going on here than just business? Was there even the slightest possibility of something more?

She'd caught a glimpse of him in her peripheral vision. His hair barely touched his ears. Light from the chandelier accented blond streaks in his sandy-brown hair. Okay, so he was attractive, intelligent and he was a good dad.

But even when he was joking with the kids, his smile would fade and that indefinable shadow settled into his expression. Then he managed a much more artificial smile, one that didn't show in his eyes. Although she was drawn to him, she thought it best to keep this relationship just friendly. There must be things he was dealing with she couldn't begin to understand or fix. That was God's job.

When she stepped out of the elevator, she saw Quinton. He was facing her door, leaning against the opposite wall while he wrote on a piece of paper. As always, Quinton looked as if he'd fallen out of the pages of an upscale men's catalog.

His eyes brightened when he noticed her. "There you are. I was just leaving a note to let you know I stopped by."

"You were at the fair all day. Why didn't you come over and say hi to me then?" The irritation in her voice surprised her. He hadn't come by to say hello to her and that hurt. Despite what she told herself, she still had feelings for him.

"I was working the room. Making contacts, et cetera, et cetera." Quinton ran his hands over his wavy blond hair.

"Find any new talent?"

"None as gifted as you." He reached out and touched

her cheek. "I miss you, Tasha. I sit in church by my-self every Sunday."

The warmth of his touch lingered on her face even after he pulled his hand away. Quinton was a man Tasha should have been proud to take home to meet her mother. He was successful, handsome, hardworking and, above all, a Christian. Yet Tasha had always felt as if there was something missing from their relationship, though she could never quite put her finger on it. The number of hours he spent working had always been a point of conflict for them—but there was something else that just didn't feel right, despite the qualities in his favor that should have made him a perfect match.

Tasha swallowed hard, trying to dismiss the stir of mixed-up emotions she felt. "Thank you for stopping by. It was good to see you again." She struggled to keep her voice neutral. The veil between affection and anger was thin, and right now she was wrestling with both.

She pulled her key card out of her pocket, swiped it in the slot and pushed open the door.

As she stepped into her room, she heard his foot-steps on the carpet behind her. "I thought maybe we could go out for coffee."

Tasha spun around. "I've made other plans, Quinton. Thanks." There really was no such thing as mak-ing a clean break in a relationship. He was stirring up old emotions. Feelings she could keep at bay as long as she was a twelve-hour drive away from him.

"What plans?"

"I'm meeting—" She kicked off her loafers. "Quinton, it's none of your business. We're not dating any-more."

He picked up one of the dolls she had left behind

to be repaired. "Even if you don't want me to be part of your life, our sales at Newburg Designs have been down since you left." He held the doll by one leg and pointed it at her. "Maybe when you get done playing with dolls, you'll come back."

Rising tension, triggered by indecision, made the back of her neck tighten and her temples throb. It would be so easy to come back. Then she wouldn't have all these bills hanging over her head. "I'm not playing with dolls, Quinton. What I do is meaningful." This was one of the reasons they'd broken up. He was utterly unsupportive of her dream. He ridiculed it. "When I was working for Newburg's slave factory, nothing was ever mine. I had no control. Newburg was always re-working my ideas."

"If that's all it's about, maybe I could just talk to her."

"No, no, it's more than that, Quinton. I want my work to mean something, to help people. I don't want to make clothes for self-indulgent, rich women."

"Making dolls helps people?" His mouth curled slightly—almost a sneer.

She thought about showing him the picture of Mary and her mother, but trying to explain this to Quinton felt useless. She had already tried a hundred times to get him to understand. "Just go, Quinton, please."

He looked at her with blue-gray eyes, his gaze unwavering. "If that's what you want, Tasha." He tossed the doll back on the dresser. "Newburg says to remind you to come by the office before you leave. She has a surprise for you."

"I know. She told me." What could Newburg's surprise possibly be? It must be big if she had told Quinton to remind her. "I'll come by the office on Monday, early."

"Maybe we could do brunch."

"No, Quinton. I really need to get back home. I lose workdays when I do a craft fair."

"Don't tell me you actually have that many orders to fill." Quinton crossed his arms.

Tasha felt like throwing a pillow at him. Okay, so she didn't have endless piles of work to do because everyone wanted her dolls. It was still mean of Quinton to point it out. "Why don't you just go, Quinton?" Tasha rested her forehead in her open palm.

"Tasha, I'm trying to help you." He reached out and grabbed her arm. "The number one rule of business is if you are not making money, do something else."

Tasha pulled away from his touch. "It's not about money. It's about doing what I love." Quinton stared blankly at her. She could talk until she was blue in the face; he would never understand. "Just go, please."

He left without another word. She heard his feet brushing the carpet and the door clicking shut. Tasha plopped down on the bed and stared at the doll in her arms. Brown glass eyes gazed up at her. She brushed a golden strand of hair off the doll's face.

Maybe Quinton was right. Maybe she was just being foolish. She had spent months praying before she gave notice at Newburg Designs. And moving back to Pony Junction allowed her to be close to her seventy-year-old mom. Was she wrong in thinking that making dolls was what God wanted her to do?

She opened her purse and pulled out the picture Philip had given her. If her design could provide comfort for Mary, that would make it all worthwhile. She placed the picture on a nightstand.

Pushing herself up off the bed, she unbuttoned her flowing blue dress and slipped into a pair of jeans and a purple jewel-neck blouse. After a quick glance at herself in the mirror and a little lip gloss, she headed upstairs to the pool.

Chapter 4

The pool was on the top floor with floor-to-ceiling glass walls that looked out on the city. When Tasha stepped across the threshold, wet heat settled on her skin and the scent of chlorine hung in the air. The snowstorm muted the twinkling lights from buildings. Through the steamy windows, she could just make out the outline of skyscrapers and the random blue glow from windows.

Besides Philip's family, there were only a few other people at the pool. An older couple sat in lounge chairs in matching yellow bathrobes. The woman, wet hair matted to her head, leaned back against her headrest and closed her eyes. She reached over and patted her sleeping husband's arm. Another man swam laps in the far lane. His face turned toward Tasha and then away in a blur of motion and water. Triangular elbows jutted out of the water at precise intervals.

Grace looked up from the magazine she was flipping through and waved Tasha over with a big toothy grin. "Have a seat." She tugged at the unzipped sage-green terry cover-up so it hid her hips and stomach.

The white plastic lounge chair creaked when Tasha sat down.

Philip roughhoused with the boys by letting them stand on his hands and then tossing them in the water. The two girls floated around on a single inner tube, kicking idly, giggling and pressing their heads close together.

Grace glanced out at the pool. "He's so good with kids. Too bad he won't have any more."

"He's young. He might marry again."

"A few months ago, he thought he was ready to start dating." Grace shook her head. "Believe me, there were plenty of women standing in line. Everybody wants to date 'the doctor'—needy, desperate women. I think he got tired of it." Grace closed her magazine. "He likes you."

"Me?" Grace's candor caught Tasha off guard. "I barely know him."

Grace patted Tasha's leg. "I saw the way he looked at you at dinner. A sister knows these things."

"I'm flattered. But I'm trying to get a business off the ground. I don't have time for a relationship." Certainly not with someone who lived twelve hours away. She glanced at Philip as he held his hands close to his face to block splashing water. The acoustics of the pool room accentuated the rich bass tones of his laughter.

Grace responded to her protests by raising one eyebrow and drawing her lips into a straight line. She sighed. "I think the whole dating thing just made him miss Heather more."

"How did she die?"

"Philip probably didn't tell you that part. It's hard for him to talk about it. She had pancreatic cancer. She was only ill for a short time, but I think because he was a doctor, he thought he should have been able to do more."

Lost in thought, Tasha settled back into the lounge chair. "How's he doing now?"

Grace sat up straighter. "Ever since Heather died, he's been working more and more hours at the clinic." Grace stared out at the pool. "I'm just a big sister. I can't tell him anything. But he's drowning his sorrow in work. He's not dealing with it."

Philip and the boys sent up a huge spray of water. Tasha laughed as it sprinkled her jeans.

"Hey, watch it. You got water drops all over my magazine," Grace taunted.

"Would you like some cheese with that whine? You poor baby. Why don't you jump in the pool and get even?" Philip chided.

The boys joined in. "Come and get us, Mom. Come and get us."

Grace stood up and took her robe off. "I think I will." She ran for the pool and did a huge, splashing cannonball. The eruption of water was followed by a burst of protest from the children, screaming, "Oh, Mom!"

"I'm so embarrassed." Damaris slapped her cheeks with her hands, rolled her eyes and shook her head.

"You think that was embarrassing…" Grace proceeded to splash water on her daughter and Mary. The two girls jumped off the tube and joined in the water fight.

Tasha watched. "Now I wish I'd brought my suit."

"You're missing out on all the fun," Philip yelled in between dodging water bullets.

Tasha shook her head. What a wonderful family. Would her life have been different if she'd had siblings? Being an only child had given her lots of time to develop her artistic abilities. Dolls had been her best friends. Maybe that was why she liked them so much. Still, it would have been nice to have a brother to protect her or a sister to play dress-up with.

About half an hour later, everyone crawled out of the pool. The three other people had already left.

Philip toweled his wet hair. He looked at his sister and cocked his head to one side, which Tasha took as some kind of signal between siblings. "Grace, why don't you take the kids downstairs? I'll join you in a minute."

Grace picked up on the signal and gathered the kids together. As the children ran ahead of her out of the pool room, she caught Tasha's arm just above the elbow. "Listen, if you need some fabric for your dolls, I can sell some to you at cost. I stocked up on it when I became delusional and thought I had the talent to be a professional quilter."

"Actually, any supplies I can get wholesale are worth it. Maybe I can stop by your place sometime."

Philip waited until Grace was out the door before addressing Tasha. "I have more photos at home if they would help you make the dolls."

"The photo you gave me will be a good start. But

anything that shows other facial angles would be helpful."

"You'll have them done by Christmas?" He swung his towel over his shoulders.

"I should be able to get them done a few weeks before." She leaned a little closer and touched his arm. "I thought I was going to spend the night alone with the television. Thank you for inviting me to dinner. You have a wonderful family. I like your sister."

"She's all right for a big sister. After—after Heather died—Grace, well, she—" He wiped a wet spot on his arm with his towel. "Well, let's just say she's the strong one in the family."

Philip's grief over his wife still seemed very close to the surface. Not wanting to say anything that would aggravate his sorrow, Tasha remained silent.

They sauntered out of the pool room and down the hall together. "Thank you for doing this for Mary."

"Custom-made dolls are my favorites."

They lingered in the hallway. Grace's words—*He likes you*—floated into her mind. Tasha took a step back. Best not do anything to encourage a pointless relationship. This was business—just business.

His wet hair was slicked back from his face, making his brown eyes stand out even more. Tasha took a second step back. "What floor are you on?"

"Just down one flight."

As they walked down the hall and to the stairs together, she couldn't help but sneak a glance at him. There it was again, that sad look in his eyes. Philip was enduring an ache that she could not possibly hope to assuage.

They walked down the hallway, exchanging small talk, until they stood outside Grace's hotel room.

Tasha could hear the laughter of the children from inside the room. If they were anything like she was as child, staying at a hotel was the most fascinating thing in the world. The kids probably wouldn't go to bed for a long time.

A little body banged against the partially open door. Tasha smiled. "I hope you don't have to work tomorrow. You're probably not going to get much sleep."

"I always try to take Sunday off. We can catch the late service at church. I have to work a lot of hours, but since—" Again, the awkward pause. "I try to spend as much time with Mary as I can."

"She's a sweet girl."

Philip's face brightened and he grinned. "Thank you." He was definitely a daddy.

Tasha said goodbye, promising to keep him informed about her progress on the dolls.

When she got to her room, Tasha gazed out at the city. The blizzard had let up a bit, and she could see the glow and twinkle of Christmas lights everywhere.

It would be good to spend a leisurely Christmas with Mom. When she was working for Newburg Designs, she was lucky if she had time to say hello to her mother before she had to turn around and drive back to Denver.

Without her substantial salary from Newburg, she wouldn't be able to buy her mother the lavish gifts she had loved to give her. Her mother would be happy with any gift—that was not what Christmas was about for them. Still, Tasha liked the thrill of seeing Mom's face when she opened a box and saw a one-of-a-kind leather purse or imported perfume. Mom had always been frugal. Tasha liked spoiling her.

She sighed and plopped down on the hotel bed, idly tracing the floral design of the bedspread. When she was working for Newburg, she had lots of money but no time, and now she had lots of time to spend with people she loved, but money was always a worry.

As she gazed at the doll propped up beside the TV set and thought of the mounting bills waiting for her at home, she wondered if she had made the right trade-off.

At the sound of Mary's crying, Philip's eyes fluttered open. Grace and the kids were in the adjoining room. Mary had wanted to do a sleepover with her cousins, but he knew the bad dreams and crying would wake everyone and embarrass Mary.

He slipped out of his bed and walked over to her bed without turning on the light.

He stroked her forehead. "Mary, it's Daddy. You're having a bad dream." He gathered her into his arms and rocked her back and forth, humming a soft lullaby until she quieted. He stroked her head and held her a moment longer before laying her on her side and covering her with the blanket.

She stirred but did not wake. He retrieved Mr. Happy from the end of the bed and lifted her arm and placed the stuffed cat so Mary could hold it while she slept.

Unable to go back to sleep himself, he slumped down in a chair and sat in the darkness. If he turned on a light to read, he might wake Mary. He rose and

tiptoed across the room, opening the door to the adjoining room slightly.

He doubted Mary would wake up again, but if she
did, Grace would hear her. He grabbed a book and
headed down to the fifth floor, where he knew there
was a quiet lounge. He'd been to medical conferences
here and had found the lounge when he needed a moment away from the crowds and the constant shoptalk.
He put on his robe and grabbed the bag of cookies
Grace had made for him. Stepping into the hall, he
made sure the door was locked behind him.

As expected, the lounge was empty. It was three
o'clock in the morning. Who else would be up at
this hour anyway? He sat down in one of the comfy
couches.

He stared down at the book he'd grabbed and realized what he really needed to do was pray. No matter
how many times he picked up on the sadness in Mary's
expression or how many times she woke up crying, his
concern for her never diminished. He'd give anything
to take the hurt away from his little girl. He had such
hope for the dolls Tasha was going to make.

He knew that it wouldn't just be one thing that
helped Mary heal. Mary had been so young when
Heather died. The little girl's memories were not that
clear. Some of this pain was connected to not having
a mom at all. He saw the look on Mary's face when
the other moms came to her friends' school perfor-
mances or picked their kids up. Not having a mom
wasn't something he could fix, even if he was the best
dad in the world.

He heard footsteps outside the lounge, and Tasha appeared in the doorway. She looked kind of cute in her

bathrobe with cats and kittens on it and fuzzy bunny slippers. He smiled at her. "I thought I was the only one who knew about this place."

"I used to do fashion shows here. I found this place one afternoon when I needed a break from the chaos," she said.

Something else they had in common. They both needed downtime. He scooted over on the couch to make room for her.

She sat down beside him. "How do you know about this lounge? And what are you doing up this late?"

"Question number one—I've been to a dozen medical conventions in this hotel." He breathed in the light floral scent of Tasha's perfume. "Question number two—I could ask you the same thing."

"I couldn't sleep, so I came out here to pray." She pulled a bag of candy out of her bathrobe pocket. "I come bearing gifts. I stopped at a vending machine and it turns out they had some of that wonderful taffy from that candy shop downtown." When he glanced down at the floor, she slipped her bunny-clad feet farther under the coffee table. It was kind of endearing that she was trying to hide them. He had already seen the savvy businesswoman side of her. It was nice to know she had a playful side, as well.

"I love taffy. Here's my contribution to this snack-fest." He pulled a plastic bag filled with cookies out of his pocket. "Grace loads me up with homemade cookies every time she comes."

"Those look good. Hold out your hand and I'll give you some taffy." She placed her hand under his and sprinkled out several pieces of candy. A spark of energy zinged through him when she touched his hand.

Against his better judgment, his pulse raced. Hadn't he already told himself this was just a business relationship?

Philip met her gaze as she pulled her hand away. He looked down, pointing at her feet. "Cute slippers."

Tasha settled back into the couch. "The last person who was impressed by my slippers was ten years old."

"I find it interesting that someone who knows a lot about fashion gravitates toward fuzzy bunny slippers." She was not a predictable person. He liked that. He couldn't hide the attraction he felt for her.

She smiled and golden light came into her eyes. She reached across the table. Her shoulder brushed against his. "I'll try one of those cookies."

He took the fastener off the bag and handed her a cookie. He scooted over on the couch and leaned closer to her. "I have to warn you. You can't eat just one. They're that good." He unwrapped a piece of taffy and popped it into his mouth.

Tasha took a bite of the oatmeal cookie. She closed her eyes as she chewed. "That is a good cookie. It's nice to meet someone who is not opposed to late-night snacking."

"We're a matched set." He snatched a cookie off the coffee table.

Tasha wrinkled her forehead, obviously confused by his remark.

What an odd thing to say. They weren't a matched anything. What on earth had made him say something like that?

Regretting the impulsiveness of the remark, he cleared his throat and stared at the coffee table as if the pattern of the grain fascinated him.

"Now you have to tell me why you're really up here." Tasha selected an orange taffy.

He planted his elbows on his knees and ran his hand through his hair. "Mary was having another one of her bad dreams. So I held her until she went to sleep. By then, I was too awake to go back to bed." His voice was thick with emotion, but he felt comfortable sharing with her.

She leaned forward and put a supportive hand on his wrist. "I hope the dolls help."

"Me, too. Me, too." Resting his chin on his hands, he gazed at the wall.

"You need cheering up." Tasha perused her taffy and picked up a green one. "Close your eyes and guess what flavor this one is." She placed the unwrapped taffy in his hand after he closed his eyes.

He popped it in his mouth. After he chewed for a moment, he said, "Pistachio."

"Good guess. Most people don't get that one," Tasha said.

He pulled another cookie out of the bag and placed it in her hand. Their fingers touched briefly. "The chocolate ones are the best." Again, his heart drummed from the warmth of her touch.

Tasha took a bite of the cookie. "Maybe your sister should give up organic farming and go into the cookie-making business."

"Only if she figures out how to keep the kids from eating the inventory."

She laughed. "I like you, Philip. You have a wonderful sense of humor."

His smile faded, and he gazed at Tasha as an uncomfortable silence settled in the room. Something had definitely shifted between them.

Philip cleared his throat and looked away. "So how is life in the doll business?" Back to a safe subject. He smoothed out his tousled hair.

"Slow and kind of scary. I quit my real job eight months ago to do this full time. Thinking about the business is what woke me up in the middle of the night."

"I think what you do is admirable." He took a bite of cookie.

"Really?"

"Sure, every woman has a little girl inside her. You bring out that little girl."

"Yes, exactly." She nodded her head. "It's so nice to meet someone who understands that."

He liked the way her face became animated when she talked about her work. "So business is not so good?"

Tasha sighed and stared at the floor. "They say any business takes five years to become profitable. I just don't know if I should have given up my steady income at the design firm." She balled her hands into a fist and then stretched her fingers out. "But I needed to move back closer to Mom. She's getting older." She massaged the back of her neck. "I don't know what to do to get this business going. Christmas is the optimal time to make that happen."

An idea popped into his head. "Can you do huggable cloth dolls? The kind a kid would like."

"I can do cloth, porcelain, any kind of doll you want."

"I've spend some time at a children's hospital, and

my nurse and I volunteer at a kids' shelter. We deal with kids who are facing cancer or a battery of tests or have just been taken away from their parents. Didn't you say those were situations where a doll would be a comfort?" He knew in proposing the deal he was looking for an excuse to see her more.

Tasha lifted her head. "A doll might just be what they need to feel safe."

"Exactly. Of course, you would have to be paid. I'll have to see if I can scare up some grant money."

"You would do that for me? You barely know me," she said.

"God sent people to help me through medical school when I didn't have two dimes to rub together. I figure that I pay back all those people who helped me by helping others," he said.

"That's a neat way of looking at it." Admiration shone in her eyes. "Let's finish these snacks."

They ate and talked and laughed until only two pieces of taffy were left.

Tasha stared down at the last pieces of candy. "I guess the party's over," she said with mock sadness.

Philip studied the remaining candy. "They look kind of lonely there, don't they?" He shook his head with exaggerated drama.

"I'll take the blue one. You can have the burgundy one." She picked up the blue taffy and brought it toward her mouth.

"Wait just a minute." He grabbed her wrist to stop her. "I think I'm getting the raw end of a deal here. Do you even know what flavor the burgundy one is?"

"No." She held the blue taffy to her chest. "I always called it gobbledygook flavor. I think they put what-

ever they have left over at the end of a batch to make
the burgundy ones."

"My point exactly. But that blueberry one. Now, that
is a prize piece of candy."

"Oh, all right." With exaggerated pathos, she
slapped the blue candy down on the table.

"Now you made me feel bad. You have it." He
slumped his shoulders and hung his head theatrically
as he pushed the candy toward her.

"After that kind of protest, you take it." She slid the
single candy across the table.

"I insist." He picked up the blue taffy and placed it
in her palm, closing her fingers around it. "You take
the blueberry." He held her hand in his a little longer
than was necessary to make his point.

"Fine." She unwrapped the candy and shoved it in
her mouth.

Philip opened his mouth wide, feigning shock. "You
go right ahead and have that succulent, juicy blueberry." He stuck out his lower lip in a mock pout. "I'll
just have blah burgundy." He fluttered his eyelashes.

Tasha mimed playing a violin. "Oh, you poor baby.
Where did you learn how to tease like that?"

"Grace is my older sister. I also have two younger
sisters."

She laughed. "So you were probably tormenting
women from the day you were born."

"Hey, I was in a house full of women. It was sur-
vival." The conversation faded back into silence.

Tasha stared at the floor and smiled. She let out a
heavy sigh. "I think I'm finally tired again."

"Am I that boring?"

"No." She gave him a friendly punch in the shoul-

der. "It's not that. I have to be up in a few hours."
Stretching, she rose to her feet. "Are you going back
to your room?"

"I think I'll steal your idea and stay and pray for
a while." He twisted an empty candy wrapper in his
hands.

"All right. I'll be in touch with you about the dolls.
You can swing by and get that order form." She slipped
around the corner and was gone.

Philip settled back on the couch, shaking his head.
That was the most he had laughed in a long time. He'd
forgotten how wonderful it could be to talk to someone
who was so easy to be around.

What an unexpected surprise.

He liked Tasha. He would admit that. But some part
of him still held back. He stared down at the candy
wrappers on the coffee table and remembered how he
and Heather used to love to share a bag of cinnamon
bears.

Chapter 5

Tasha sat for a long time in her van, staring at the glittery Newburg Designs sign. Four-foot-high letters in a flourish of silver, gold and hot pink were mounted on the squarish roof of the renovated warehouse that contained the offices and factory of her former employer. Unexpected anxiety about returning to Newburg Designs corseted her stomach and rib cage. Newburg and Quinton's comments haunted her. Still, she was hopeful Newburg's promised "surprise" would be some vote of support for her business.

Tasha stared out the window down the busy street. Cars navigated through fresh snow turned to dirty slush from tires and exhaust. Christmas lights flashed in the windows of the businesses all up and down the block. Shoppers spilled out of stores onto the glistening sidewalk.

Newburg Designs was in the Historic Lower Downtown District of Denver. LoDo, as the locals called it, consisted of many renovated warehouses that had been turned into art galleries, high-end clothing stores, offices and restaurants. The boutique where Newburg sold most of their designs was four blocks away.

Early that morning, she'd packed up her own unsold dolls, dismantled her display units, checked out of the hotel and driven across town. Though she did not see Philip again in the remaining days of the craft fair except when he stopped by briefly to pick up the order form, her thoughts had returned often to him and their late-night snack session. Was his generous offer to find grant money for her only about helping her with her business? Tasha kicked herself mentally. She needed to quit trying to read some coded romantic message into everything he did. Still, she couldn't get past Grace saying that Philip liked her. And she couldn't get past the electric warmth she felt when he was close.

Philip's laughter and gentle voice echoed in her mind. *Be still, my stupid beating heart.* He was a client, that was all. Besides, with so much distance between them, a relationship would be impractical. Still, Philip was fun. Kind of like a big brother. That was it. He was a client and the sibling she'd never had. Nothing more.

Tasha gripped the steering wheel and let out a deep breath. A puffy gust of air appeared and faded quickly.

Snow fell silently to the ground. Ten minutes ago, Tasha had turned off her motor, her heater and her wipers, fully intending to jump out of her van and run inside.

Ten minutes and she still hadn't worked up the guts

to face the people at Newburg Designs and get the last boxfuls of her old life. Snow accumulated on her windshield, blurring the letters of the sign.

She thought of the sign she'd painted herself for her new business—foot-high block letters in shades of blue. She could picture the sign leaning against the side of the barn she'd renovated into a studio. She hadn't had time to mount it yet.

Tasha glanced through the side window, where she saw Quinton's Lexus in his reserved parking space. Had they already assigned her parking space to someone else?

She tapped the door handle. Cecily Newburg had said she had a surprise for her. Curiosity and hope motivated Tasha to push open the door of her van and hop down from the high seat. The chilling wind hit her hard, and she thanked God for long underwear, down coats and turtlenecks. You don't grow up in the Rocky Mountains and not know how to dress for glacial weather, even in the city.

She walked past her old parking space. The sign read Reserved for Octavia Monroe. Tasha giggled. That had to be a made-up name. She had loved the creative part of designing clothes, but the posturing and pretending that took place in the fashion industry had always made her uncomfortable.

She shoved her ungloved hands into the warm, deep pockets of her down coat and walked toward the large metal doors of the warehouse. She opened the door to a bustle of activity. The outside of Newburg Designs was deceptive. No one would guess from looking at the windowless metal building that it contained such sophisticated and lavish decor.

Inside the building, the metal walls had been dry-walled and painted hot pink, Newburg's signature color. The main floor housed the cutting tables and seamstress's stations. A balcony and railing surrounded the upstairs offices. Mannequins, some with fabric draped over them and others wearing garments that were turned inside out, populated the factory floor. Bolts of fabric lined the far wall. Several fitting models stood by the seamstress stations as women with pincushions on their wrists readjusted the garments the models wore.

"You would think they would at least remember my Savior." Tasha turned at the sound of the familiar voice. "It is Christmas after all." A roundish, four-foot-nothing woman knelt at the base of a Christmas tree arranging a nativity scene. An open box sat on the floor beside her. "Does anything about this tree say birth of a Savior to you, Tasha?" The woman addressed Tasha as though they'd been in the middle of a conversation.

Tasha looked up at the ornate ten-foot tree. A hundred silver bows, all exactly alike, and a flashing silver star decorated the tree. A string of silver beads wound its way around the tree from top to bottom. "Not really. How are you, Bernadette?"

Bernadette rose to her feet. She wore black pants, a black shirt and a red-rose–print blazer. Tasha had always referred to the outfit as Bernadette's uniform. The head seamstress for Newburg Designs always wore black with some sort of brightly colored jacket or big shirt. "Good to have you back."

Tasha said, "I'm just here to pick up the rest of my stuff."

"Of course you are." Bernadette's brown eyes shone

behind plastic-framed glasses. A bubble of gray hair, solid as a statue, was accented with a red barrette. "Let me walk you to the stairs, honey." Bernadette stood on tiptoe and whispered in Tasha's ear, "A word of warning. Newburg may try to talk you into coming back. Stand your ground." Tasha had to bend toward Bernadette to hear her, the woman was so petite.

Tasha's shoulders drooped. She shook her head. "Sometimes I wonder if I shouldn't come back."

Bernadette stopped and narrowed her eyes at Tasha. "Swallow your words right now, young lady." She patted Tasha's shoulder. "You left to pursue your dream."

"I mean it, Bernadette. I might know a lot about designing dolls, but I don't know anything about business."

Bernadette put chubby hands on her hips. "So it gets a little bit hard and you're just going to give up?"

"I know, but I—"

Bernadette held up a warning finger. "No whining. Just ask God what He is trying to teach you through this struggle."

"I guess I expected more success by now." Tasha ran her fingers through her curly hair. "Did you always want to be a seamstress? Did you always want to work for Newburg?" Bernadette had the distinction of not having missed a day of work at Newburg Designs in the ten years she'd been head seamstress.

"No, but this job pays well enough and frees me up so I can do what God wants me to do."

"How are the Christmas boxes for the orphans going this year?"

"We shipped over a thousand boxes last week. We'll get another thousand before Christmas. And next year,

Charlie and I will be able to go over to South Korea to help out for at least a month."

"Maybe that's what God wants me to do. Work at a good-paying job and use the money to help others," Tasha said.

"Sorry, that's my dream. You were called to be a doll maker."

"But I don't have the money I owe the contractors—"

Bernadette held up the warning finger again and drew her lips into a straight line. "No whining. Just trust—"

"Tasha, darling. You're here." A voice rang out from the top of the stairs. Cecily Newburg, dressed in a hot pink sheath with fur at the ends of long sleeves and around the collar, motioned for Tasha to come up the stairs.

Bernadette said, "There will always be naysayers and dream killers in the world. The trick is not to listen to them."

"Do come up here and see your surprise." Newburg's voice was lilting and singsongy, very theatrical. "Visit with me for a little bitty."

Bernadette patted Tasha on the back and winked. "Good luck, kiddo."

Newburg minced her way down the metal stairs on four-inch heels. Today Newburg's hair was candy-apple red and pulled off her face with a gold headband. She held a sheer pink rectangular scarf in her hand. "I've been waiting all morning for you. Come, come, darling. See your surprise."

Tasha walked behind Newburg to the top of the stairs. What could Newburg possibly be this excited about? Tasha's boots sank into the plush carpet of the hallway that led to the offices.

Newburg waved the scarf playfully. "Close your eyes."

"You're going to blindfold me?"

Newburg scooted around behind Tasha. "Come on, close your eyes. Have a little fun."

The sheer fabric of the scarf pressed softly against Tasha's eyelids. "This surprise must really be something." Tasha felt a tug at the back of her head. Certainly Cecily wouldn't go to all this trouble just for a box of fabric scraps. The floral scent of Newburg's perfume intensified. Noise from the factory floor seemed to get louder.

Cecily's hands pressed into Tasha's shoulders as her voice chimed from behind her. "Okay, now, I'm going to guide you. Take about ten steps this way."

Tasha tried to remember the layout of the upper floor, not an easy task with one of her senses disabled.

"Four more steps this way. Good."

Near as she could tell, they were walking roughly in the direction of her old office. A turnaround from Newburg, a vote of support, would be such a welcome blessing. *Think hopeful thoughts. Think hopeful thoughts.* A door creaked open. The faint scent of cinnamon drifted up to her nose. And what was that other smell—fresh paint?

Newburg turned Tasha's body slightly and Tasha heard a bubbling sound like water flowing over rocks.

Cecily pressed her lips close to Tasha's ear. "Are you ready?"

"Oh, I'm ready." Tasha's heart pounded in anticipation. What on earth could Newburg have for her?

Newburg made a drum roll noise as she untied Tasha's scarf. "Ta-da!" She squeezed Tasha's shoulder. "What do you think?"

Tasha gazed into what had been her old cubbyhole of an office.

"We knocked a wall out."

"The old storage room?" Disappointment flooded through her. This was definitely not a vote of support for Tasha's Dolls. It was a bribe to get her to come back to Newburg Designs.

Newburg dashed into the office. "I've got some cider brewing." That explained the cinnamon scent. Newburg waltzed around the new office, pointing out its features like Vanna White presenting consonants. "You have your own espresso machine. And look at this—a new heater. No more wearing a coat while you work at the computer."

Shaking her head, Tasha took a step into her old office. "Cecily, I—" The office had been expanded from an eight-by-eight cell to almost double that size. In the corner, a tiny fountain bubbled over smooth round stones. An abstract painting hung on the wall, one of Newburg's favorite local artists, not Tasha's.

"So what do you think?" Newburg beamed. She laced her hands together and raised her eyebrows. "Is it fabulous or what?"

Tasha glanced around. Newburg had placed a microwave close to her old desk. A huge framed photo of a model in one of Tasha's award-winning evening gowns hung behind the desk. "This must have cost a lot…to remodel."

"Don't worry about it." Newburg poured cider from

a teapot and handed the steaming mug to Tasha. "You still haven't told me what you think."

Tasha swallowed as her stomach tightened. The scent of cinnamon and apple rose from the mug. She didn't want to hurt Newburg's feelings. But she had never asked for a different office, never said that would be a condition of her staying at the job. "I think…I think…that this will be a very nice office for Octavia." Tasha spoke as gently as she could, almost whispering.

Newburg's mouth fell open. She moved several pens on Tasha's old desk, arranging them in a straight line. "Octavia is not going to last. I'm offering the job to you before I do another job search." She looked up from the desk, her eyes intent on Tasha. "We'd love to have you back, Tasha."

Tasha closed her eyes and took in a deep breath. "Cecily, this is a really wonderful office." She took the few steps to where Newburg leaned against the desk. "But it's not my office anymore." Tasha touched Newburg's shoulder. "My job and my life are in Pony Junction now."

Newburg pulled away from Tasha's touch. "You can't tell me that business is booming."

Tasha's jaw tightened. "It takes a while for a business to get a solid start. Of course, as a businesswoman, you know that." She tried not to sound defensive. But Newburg was rubbing salt in open wounds. *I don't need someone to remind me that my business is not succeeding.*

"I can offer you a ten percent pay raise."

"Cecily, I—"

"I don't understand you, Tasha. Why would someone give up a good-paying job and move to a town that doesn't even have a mall?" Newburg wrinkled her nose. "Oh, yes. Because God told you to." Her voice dripped with sarcasm.

Tasha set the cup down on the desk so hard that the amber liquid splashed out. She shook her head. It was one thing to ridicule her new job, but now Newburg was making fun of her faith. "I didn't ask for this office. You can find another designer."

Newburg turned her back to Tasha. "You are wasting your talent. This offer won't be open for much longer."

Quinton cleared his throat as he stood in the doorway with a stack of papers and a clipboard in his hand. "So what do you think of your new office, Tasha?" The blond hair and deep tan made him look as though he'd just put down his surfboard and stepped off the beach. She had always found him physically attractive, but Tasha knew that the only place to get a tan in Denver this time of year was in a tanning booth.

She narrowed her eyes at Newburg's back. "It's not my office." She took several deep breaths to calm down.

Quinton's gaze went from Tasha to Newburg and back to Tasha. He spoke haltingly. "We were just hoping—"

Tasha was so upset, words spilled out of her mouth. "I gave notice. I kept my commitments and fulfilled my contract. I finished all the holiday designs before I left. This is not my job anymore."

Quinton shoved one hand into the pocket of his gray slacks. "We had to make one final offer. You were an asset to this company."

"I didn't want us to part like this. I wanted us to remain friends," Tasha pleaded.

Quinton stared at the floor. Newburg turned around, glared at Tasha and then spoke to Quinton. "Was there some reason you came in here, Quinton?"

Tasha sighed. Newburg was doing her "you're invisible, I can't see you, Tasha" routine.

Quinton's left eyelid ticked, always a sign that he was nervous. "It can wait."

"Tell me, Quinton." Newburg crossed her arms over her chest.

Quinton held up the papers. "I wanted to talk to you about these expansion ideas. I don't know if our designs will appeal to middle America."

"Isaac Mizrahi did it. Vera Wang did it. Why can't I?"

"I'll run it by the accountant, but I don't think we have the capital. Even if we do, we only have this one factory."

Newburg let out a loud gust of air. "Just do the PR and advertising, Quinton. Let me determine the direction this company goes."

Tasha cleared her throat. "I came for the last boxes of my stuff." As she'd already told Newburg, she didn't want to part on these terms, but she wasn't going to bow to Newburg's manipulations, either.

Newburg glared at Tasha. "They are by your...by *the* desk."

"Thank you," Tasha whispered. The tension in the air was palpable.

Quinton said, "I'll help you carry them out, Tasha." He set the clipboard on the desk.

Newburg strutted toward the door. "The offer won't

be open much longer, Tasha." She stood in the hallway. "You're throwing your life away."

In a futile effort to get rid of the tightness close to her heart, Tasha took in a deep breath.

Out in the hallway, Newburg yelled at somebody down on the factory floor.

Tasha placed two large boxes on top of the desk. "I'm sorry it had to end this way, Quinton."

Quinton grinned as he picked up one of the boxes. "You know Newburg."

"Yeah, I know Newburg." Boy, did she know New-burg. Tasha glanced around the luxurious office on her way out. No, putting up with Newburg's hot/cold mood swings was not worth the pleasure of working in an office like this.

Five minutes later, Quinton closed the back doors of Tasha's van. He stood in the November cold, rub-bing his arms.

"You should have put a coat on." Quinton's wavy blond hair shone in the early afternoon sun. It was that look of casual perfection that had first attracted Tasha to him.

"I'll be all right. I'm sorry about Newburg's ma-nipulative attitude." The tone of his voice was warm.

"It wasn't a surprise. I worked for her for six years, remember."

Quinton stepped toward her. "Even if you're not going to come back, maybe you and I could still be together."

"We've got a twelve-hour drive between us." She spoke gently.

A veil fell over Quinton's eyes. He shrugged and shoved his hands into his pockets. "I've got to get back inside before I freeze." His words were colder than the air.

Tasha knew that look. He was trying to hide his hurt. Maybe that was the reason Newburg and Quinton worked so well together. Quinton's moods could be just as erratic as Cecily's. One moment he could come across as arrogant and overconfident. The next, he seemed almost fragile. He did have some endearing qualities.

Tasha watched as Quinton raced back to the warehouse. She hadn't meant for anyone to be hurt by her choice. Was she being selfish for wanting to fulfill her dream, for wanting to move closer to her mother?

Tasha opened the door of her van. She had told Quinton as plainly and as tactfully as she could that there could be nothing between them. But Quinton was a salesman to the core. He simply would not hear her no.

Yes, she had cared for him. Yet a year ago, when he had suggested they become engaged, she had said no. Tasha and Quinton shared the same faith, but for some reason she couldn't view him as marriage material. Even if she had remained in Denver, she and Quinton wouldn't have stayed together.

Slamming the van door, she turned the key and waited for the engine to warm up. She felt as if birds were beating their wings against the inside of her rib cage. Tasha flipped through her collection of music and shoved an instrumental worship CD in the slot. The soft strains of an acoustic guitar filled the van. The birds fluttered less.

She drove through early-afternoon traffic and, without knowing why, took a slight detour to drive past the building where Philip's office was. She glanced at the high-rise as she waited at a red light.

Philip was nice, and Mary was adorable, but she needed to focus on making her business profitable. She sure shouldn't feed any of the feelings of attraction for Philip that had budded inside her.

The light turned green. Tasha pressed down on the accelerator, speeding toward the vast open road that led back to her new life.

Chapter 6

Philip Strathorn turned Tasha's business card over in his hand. He smiled at the pencil drawing of the Raggedy Ann doll before tossing it on his desk beside a pile of medical journals. She'd probably done the drawing herself. What a gifted woman. And fun. Any woman who wore fuzzy bunny slippers was okay in his book.

A nurse poked her head into Philip's office. "Your bronchitis is waiting in Exam 3, and Lower Back Pain says she has another question for you, Exam 5."

"Thanks, Angela." Philip sighed deeply and stared out the window. A fluffy snowfall drifted out of the sky.

Lower Back Pain always had another question for him. The woman came into his office at least twice a month reeking of perfume and looking for any excuse she could find for Philip to examine her. Her illnesses were minor or nonexistent.

He picked up Tasha's card again and held it close to his nose. It smelled like paper and ink. Why had he hoped to find Tasha's faint floral scent?

"Dr. Strathorn, is everything all right?" Nurse Angela Hargrove's gray hair was set off by green Christmas bulb earrings. A "Jesus is the Reason for the Season" pin decorated her smock.

"I'm fine…just thinking."

She turned to go.

"Hey, Ang," he said, placing Tasha's business card carefully in his top drawer, "after today, why don't you see if Dr. Belmont can take Lower Back Pain. If she protests, just tell her my caseload is heavy." Philip suspected that after a couple visits with seventy-year-old Dr. Belmont, all of Lower Back Pain's ailments would be cured.

Angela winked at him and made a gun with her finger. "Gotcha." She narrowed her eyes at him. "That wouldn't be a lie, you know, about you having a heavy caseload."

"Have you been talking to my sister?" Philip stood up, grabbed his white coat off the back of the chair and slipped into it.

Angela shrugged. "She and I are conspiring to get you to learn how to relax."

"I do know how to relax. Don't you have paperwork to fill out or something?"

Angela smiled at him and shook her head. "Or something," she chimed in. She left his office and headed down the hallway.

The phone rang just as he stepped across the threshold.

"Hey, ya big palooka. It's your sister."

"Grace, I was just talking about you." He stepped back into his office.

"Good, I hope. Gary took another truck run to Arizona, and I'm stuck in the house with three children. Very scary. Why don't you and Mary come up and participate in the nightmare?"

"You know I have to work, right?" He rested his hand on the back of the chair.

"And I also know none of those doctors would raise an eyebrow if you took a whole week off. I'm only asking for the weekend," Grace said.

"Sis, don't get started again with your pop psychology. I work because I like to work. And it's a twelve-hour drive to your place. That's not exactly a weekend kind of trip." Philip tugged at the collar of his lab coat and then sat down in his desk chair.

"So that's a no, huh?" There was a brief silence on the other end of the line. "Too bad, I was going to call Tasha and see if she wanted some of my fabric. You wouldn't happen to have her number, would you? Maybe she'll come over for dinner since my little brother is so busy."

Philip pressed the receiver close to his ear. "Grace, you're being a little too obvious." He glanced at the drawer where he'd placed Tasha's card. The mention of her name made his stomach somersault.

"Obvious? *Moi?* Does Saturday work for you? You and Mary can fly up on Friday and leave Monday. That's only two days off work. I'll drive out and meet you at the airport."

Philip sat back down in his chair. "I did say I'd give Tasha some more photos. I'll come up, but don't push, Grace. I mean it. I don't want to live through any more real-life episodes of *The Bachelor*." He swiveled his chair back and forth.

Grace's voice softened. "I hear ya. No more big-sister matchmaking."

"See you late Friday." Philip hung up the phone after giving Grace Tasha's number. He glanced back at his desk drawer where he'd tossed Tasha's card. He rose from his chair and headed down the hallway to deal with Lower Back Pain one last time.

Tasha pulled her cardigan around her shoulders. The big barn was always a little chilly, but today she was certain it was warmer outside than inside. She had only a woodstove for heat.

The scanned photograph of Mary and her mother fell out of her printer. Tasha set it up on her easel and paced back and forth, never taking her eyes off the photo. Later she would take measurements of the faces to determine how close the eyes were to each other, what the proportionality of the features ought to be on the custom-made doll. But first she needed to study the faces.

Planting her feet, she stared directly at the photo. The bodies of the dolls were just the standard adult- and child-size bodies. Since Mary would want to hold the dolls, Tasha thought a soft cloth body with a wire skeleton would be best. The individuality of her dolls came from the sculpted head and hands.

Still staring at the photograph, she picked up a mound of clay and worked it in her hands until it softened. She rolled the clay into a ball and placed it on a wooden stool she used as her sculpting space. The stool

was set up by the woodstove to keep the clay from getting too cold to work with.

Mary would be the easy head to design because
Tasha had more than a photo as a resource. Glancing up at the picture, Tasha worked the clay using her
sculpting tools to carve out a nose and eyes. Once she
got a clay head she was happy with, she could make
a mold from it. From there, she would pour porcelain
into the mold to make the head.

Tasha liked the warm, smooth texture of clay as
she worked it with her hands. Dipping her fingers in
water, she wetted the clay. She shaved off clay by the
cheeks and brought the chin to a more pronounced
point to replicate Mary's heart-shaped face. Slowly, a
form began to rise out of the clay. Her heart beat faster
as she scraped her curved molding tool over the eye
area and a lid emerged. Wiping her brow, she stood
back from her work.

This head was a rough draft at best; she'd do another
after taking measurements.

Tasha rocked back and forth, toe to heel. She loved
this process. Nothing felt as good as having her hands
covered in clay. She took in a deep breath. The tangy
pungency of paint and turpentine in her studio smelled
better than expensive perfume. She loved looking up
at the dolls lining her shelves.

Doll making let her use all her artistic talent: sculpting, painting and clothing design. How could she ever
give this up?

She shivered. The memory of her heated office at
Newburg Designs taunted her. Maybe a cup of hot tea
would warm her up. Her feet tapped on the concrete

floor as she went over to the hot plate, where she kept a full kettle of water.

She stared around at the huge barn. It had cost her savings and then some to remodel this place. Wooden beams slanted down from the roof. In the far corner, she'd built an open loft, where she slept. Below the loft was the bathroom, complete with a huge claw-foot bathtub she'd found at an estate sale. Soaking in the hot tub at the end of the day took the chill off her body and gave her time to think about her designs. Eventually, she'd get more wiring done so she could have a real stove and electric heat. But right now the hot plate was enough. She ate most of her meals at Mom's house anyway.

She pulled a tea bag out of the wrapper and placed it in a mug. She had installed a woodstove near her work area, but trying to heat the big space with wood heat was like trying to empty the ocean with a teaspoon. Buying cords of wood was proving to be costly. Maybe paying for a heating system in the first place would have been smarter.

The teakettle whistled, and she poured steaming water into her mug. It was a comfort just to hold the warm cup in her hand. Breathing in the steam, she walked back to her work area. She placed the enlarged copy of the photo on her drawing table and set a transparent grid over the faces. After eyeballing it for a moment, she put the grid aside and began to reduce the faces to a series of measurements, with lines drawn from eye to eye, from the end of the nose to the top of the mouth, from the edge of the lip to the ear.

The phone rang. Tasha let the machine pick it up.

She hated any interruption when she was working. She recognized Newburg's singsong voice right away.

"Tasha, darling, I know you're there. I have your new address and phone number now." There was a pause on the line. "Listen, I'm really sorry about the way I acted when you were here. I—I just wish you would change your mind. You and Newburg Designs were such a good fit."

Tasha laughed as the phone clicked off. Cecily Newburg spoke with an accent that sounded either French or British on any given day. Actually, Newburg was from Idaho.

Tasha recalled one of Newburg's favorite tidbits of wisdom: "Exotic and foreign sells in this town, darling. Podunk hillbilly does not." Working for Newburg had never been easy, but she had learned a great deal there. Underneath all the showiness, Cecily Newburg did have a heart.

Tasha tried to focus on her work and not think about Newburg's call or that lovely, warm, plush office back in Denver. She was grateful for Newburg's apology. Maybe things could still be repaired between them.

By lunchtime, she'd completed her measurements and had a rough sculpted rendering for both doll heads. She paced around the interior perimeter of her barn while she ate a ham sandwich. An idea brewed in her head. She had all this unused area in the barn. Why not advertise for some renters, other artists who needed studio space? With any luck, she could save enough money to get a heating system installed by next winter.

Tasha sat down at her computer and designed a poster that read Painters, Sculptors, Artists: Studio Space For Rent. She typed in her phone number and looked over the poster. Opening her home to strangers was a scary idea. She needed people who kept the same hours she did and would not distract her from her work, but she couldn't put that in the ad. While she printed copies of the poster, she prayed.

Lord, please help so the right person sees this and responds to it. Send me another believer, or if it be Your will, send somebody who needs to hear about You. Someone who doesn't keep crazy artist hours would be nice, too. I put it in Your hands.

She threw on her coat, hat and mittens and headed out the door to start her van.

Downtown Pony Junction was exactly five blocks long, but the streets bustled with Christmas shoppers. Feather-soft snowflakes drifted to the sidewalks. Christmas lights decorated bare deciduous trees, which punctuated the boulevard at intervals. The shop windows had the same glow, some with flashing red and green bulbs.

Pony Junction's brick buildings had been built around the turn of the twentieth century. Most of the old architecture had been preserved. Tasha thought that, except for the modern automobiles, these five blocks looked as though they belonged on a Currier & Ives Christmas card.

Tasha hung posters up at the hardware store and the bookstore, which also sold art supplies. She walked back to her car, got in and waited while her old van warmed up. Puffs of visible breath filled the cab as she crossed her arms over her chest. Hopefully, she would have a tenant before the New Year.

Tasha shifted into Drive. She was still plagued by doubt about this whole doll-making endeavor. She had been tempted by Newburg's offer. If she went back to Denver, there would be no more struggle…and no more shivering. She pulled out into the street. There was only one place to go when she was feeling this way.

Pressing the accelerator, she turned off the main street. After driving through a section of town with older brick homes, she saw the landscape change to open fields and cows huddled around hay bales.

Her mother had always said that people learned and were shaped not by the happy times in their lives, but by the hard times. Starting this business had been the first real risk Tasha had taken in her life. What was God trying to teach her through this hardship?

She passed a trailer park and turned down a dirt road. A little white church nearly disappeared in the field of snow as she drove toward it. The tall white spire made it look like it belonged on a Christmas card. A rough-hewn wooden cross stood in the field not far from the church.

Pastor Matthew, dressed in his dark coat and untied boots, shoveled the walkway. She pulled up beside his minivan and jumped out.

He waved and leaned on his shovel. As she approached, he spoke loudly, "Glad you came by. Gives me time to stop and catch my breath."

He was a man in his late forties with a full head of rich brown hair and clear green eyes. "How are you, Tasha?" He held one arm out to her while gripping the snow shovel with the other.

Tasha appreciated the fatherly hug. "I'm surviving."

"Sometimes that's all you can do." He craned his neck and studied her for a moment. "You've given me an excuse to rest a spell and get warmed up. Why don't you come inside for a moment? I'm sure Mindy's got some hot water on for cocoa." Jamming his shovel in the snow, he wrapped an arm around Tasha and guided her toward the church.

Both Pastor Matthew and his wife had what Tasha called the ability to look underneath someone's skin. They could see past any cheerful facade she attempted to put on, so she might as well be honest with them.

The big wooden door creaked when Pastor Matthew opened it. They stepped through the carpeted foyer and into the sanctuary. Mindy was on the stage, softly playing the piano and stopping from time to time to write on her sheet music. Her straight blond hair fell to the middle of her back. Mindy's face was one Tasha would love to sculpt because of her almond-shaped eyes and high cheekbones. Her other features were a little washed out. She wasn't beautiful in the traditional sense, but she had an inner glow that made her attractive.

"How's the nativity coming?" the pastor asked.

Tasha had volunteered to make a doll nativity for the church. "Almost done. I've just got to do the Baby Jesus."

"Yes, the all-important Jesus." He patted her back. "You do good work. It'll look nice for the Christmas Eve celebration." He glanced down at the ad for a tenant she held in her hand.

"I was hoping to put this on the bulletin board," Tasha said.

He took it from her and read it. "Still having trouble making ends meet?"

Tasha nodded. Thinking about the mounting bills and slow sales caused her throat to constrict. "I am afraid I've just been an impulsive fool. What kind of a person leaves a steady paycheck for this kind of uncertainty?"

Pastor Matthew leaned close and touched her nose. "Someone who is listening to God and trusting Him."

They walked toward the front of the church. Mindy smiled at them before returning to her playing. The pastor sat on the stairs that led up to the stage. He ran his hand through his hair. "Let's take a quiz, Miss Tasha."

Tasha sat down in the front pew. The wooden bench felt hard against her back. "Okay, quiz me."

"Do you like making dolls?"

"More than anything in the world."

"Were you happy at your old job?"

"I was miserable."

Pastor Matthew winked at her. "End of quiz. Time for cocoa."

Mindy stopped playing and giggled. "That's Matthew's version of a great philosophical discussion." She stood up. "I could use a cocoa break, too."

After talking and laughing for an hour with Pastor and Mindy, Tasha felt better. She drove home, her confidence renewed.

When she opened the creaking wooden door to the barn, the lights were on. Her mother, dressed in a purple jogging suit, leaned over Tasha's cutting table.

Elizabeth Henderson smiled up at her daughter. "I brought a casserole. It's still warm."

Tasha slipped out of her coat and hung it on a hook by the door. "I hope you didn't drive."

"Mrs. Livingston down the road brought me." Elizabeth glanced at the cutting table. Her shoulders slumped and her smile faded. The intense light and high roof of the barn made the older woman seem somehow smaller.

Tasha knew what that look meant. She raced over to her mother. "Mama, what is wrong?" Her eyes traveled to where Elizabeth's hands rested on a doll's gingham apron embroidered with a row of x's and flowers. A stack of similar aprons without embroidery rested on the table.

"I tried to finish them." The older woman's eyes misted. "But my hands."

Her mother's hands were almost translucent in the intense light. "Oh, Mama, it doesn't matter." Tasha held her mother's hand in her own. The fingers were cold and brittle as icicles.

Elizabeth whispered, "I can't get them to work anymore."

Tasha wrapped her arms around her mother. Elizabeth's cheek rested on Tasha's shoulder. "I can do the needlework. You taught me, you know."

"I wanted to help you."

Tasha stood back and held her mother's face in her hands. "You do help me. You brought me a casserole." Etchings of a lifetime showed in her mother's face, in each wrinkle, in the crow's feet, the furrows and laugh lines. Her eyes, though teary, were still as bright as Tasha remembered from childhood. "Come on, Mama. Let's eat."

As they made their way toward the card table her mother had set up, Tasha noticed her answering machine blinking that she had two messages. Had someone called about renting studio space already? She clicked the button.

The first message was the one from Newburg that she hadn't played back yet. This time she listened to the message with new ears. This was where she needed to be, helping her mother, working on her business. God would provide a way for her to pull things together financially.

The machine clicked and the second message began. "Hi, Tasha. This is Grace, Philip's sister. Philip's coming up with Mary this weekend. He said he'd bring more photos if you need them. If you want to swing by and get them, that would be great. And you can look at my fabric." She paused. "Oh, Philip gets here late Friday night. So why don't you come by for dinner on Saturday, say around six." Grace ended the message with her phone number.

Tasha shook her head. What was big sister Grace up to? Tasha could go by anytime and pick up the photos and fabric. For that matter, Philip could email her the photos. So why was Grace trying to engineer things so Tasha would come when Philip was there?

"Who's Philip?" Elizabeth lit a single taper in the middle of the table. She'd used some of Tasha's fabric, a Christmas print, as a tablecloth.

Tasha seated herself at the table. "A client. I'm making some custom dolls for him." Steam, along with the scent of cheddar, rose from the casserole dish when Tasha lifted the foil. Both women bowed their heads and Tasha said grace.

After saying, "Amen," in unison, the older woman spooned some potato-and-ham mixture onto Tasha's plate. "Is he good-looking?"

Tasha stabbed her fork through a cheese-covered potato. "Mama, don't get started."

"I'd just like some grandbabies to hold, that's all." Elizabeth's hand trembled as she lifted her fork to her mouth. The joints on the fingers were knobby and swollen.

Her mother had been joking about grandbabies since Tasha's high school graduation. In the candlelight, Elizabeth's features seemed harsher, with more contrast between the soft glow from the flame and the part of her face that was in shadow. Her lips were drawn into a straight, hard line. She was obviously trying to hide the pain in her hands.

Tasha took a bite of casserole. Somehow, tonight, the line about grandchildren didn't seem so funny.

"So are you going over there for dinner?" Elizabeth dabbed the corner of her mouth with a napkin.

"I don't want to give the wrong impression. He's a client. I need to be polite. I'll go over and get the photos, but I won't stay for dinner."

"It's your choice, dear." Elizabeth took a sip of cranberry juice.

Tasha had to admit that there was much to admire about Dr. Philip Strathorn. Anybody who liked fuzzy bunny slippers and late-night snacking was a good guy. "If you must know, yes, he is good-looking. He's also a doctor."

Elizabeth lifted her eyebrows. "Oh, well."

"Mama," Tasha scolded.

When she glanced at her shelves full of dolls and the cutting table piled with fabric, she felt her determination growing. If her business was going to succeed, it would take all her energy. A long-distance relationship with Philip Strathorn would only rob her of the time she needed to make her dream happen.

She studied her mother's bent fingers and thought of the gingham aprons on her cutting table.

"I baked brownies for dessert," Elizabeth said. The fork clattered on the plate as it fell from her hands. "Stupid arthritis." She managed a smile as she massaged her hands. "Get that worried look off your face, Tasha."

"It's getting worse, isn't it, Mama?" Tasha couldn't make her face look unconcerned. And she couldn't stop the anxiety twisting her stomach.

"It's nothing, Tasha. Eat your dinner."

Tasha wasn't hungry anymore. No matter what happened to her business, she needed to live close to her mother.

Chapter 7

Philip stood in the entryway putting on his snow pants when he saw the lights of Tasha's van coming up the driveway. The quickening of his heartbeat surprised him.

"Grace, Tasha is here."

Grace came around the corner, wiping her hands on a dish towel and slinging it over her shoulder. "You should invite her to go sledding with you and the kids." Shawn toddled around the corner and wrapped his arm around his mother's legs. His cheeks were a rosy red as he sucked on two fingers.

His sister's matchmaking could be a little over the top sometimes. "I'm sure she wouldn't be interested in that."

"It's just an idea, Philip." She lifted Shawn up into her arms. "I've got to get dinner finished up. How am

I supposed to entertain her?" She disappeared into the kitchen again.

Tasha's van eased past the organic-produce sign and parked behind Grace's SUV. Tasha killed the lights. He watched as she opened the door and headed up the sidewalk.

He clicked on the porch light for her just as she came up the stairs. He liked the way she smiled when she saw the Christmas tree through the window. He opened the door for her and was struck by how beautiful a night it was.

It got dark early in Montana in the winter. Sunset was around dinnertime, so in another twenty minutes, the sky would turn from gray to black. Already a three-quarter moon hung in a pale sky. Not a sky he'd ever seen in Denver.

His eyes traveled down to Tasha as the golden glow of the porch light washed over her. "Hey, good to see you."

She motioned to his snow pants. "Looks like you're right in the middle of something. I won't stay long. I just came to get the photos. I'm having a little trouble getting a good read on the Heather doll, so the pictures should help."

She seemed to be in a hurry. Dinner was probably Grace's idea. Tasha might not know anything about it. "Yeah, I'm headed out to go sledding with the kids. I can run and get those photos real quick." He turned and his sister was standing in the doorway of the kitchen.

"Dinner will take at least an hour. Why don't you go sledding with Philip and the kids and have a nice meal with us." He noticed that Grace deliberately didn't look at him.

Tasha glanced at her khaki pants. "But I'm not dressed—"

Grace stopped her midsentence by pulling snow pants and ski gloves off a coat rack in the entryway and placing them in Tasha's hands. "Now you're dressed. They might be a little big on you. They're mine."

She cast a nervous glance toward Philip. "Grace, I really had just intended to—"

"I insist. Go have some fun. I'll call you in when dinner is ready."

"I don't know if I'll be able to stay for dinner."

Grace raised an eyebrow. "That's no problem. Go sledding and we'll see after that."

She glanced again at Philip, who shrugged his shoulders. "Big Sis says how it's going to be around here."

Normally, it bugged him when his sister tried to fix his life, but this time he was grateful that she'd pushed a little. The thought of Tasha's not staying would have made the evening less bright.

Tasha stared down at the ski jacket. "I haven't been sledding since I was a teenager. I used to love it, though." Tasha seemed to be figuring out that any protest would be highly ineffective against Grace and her plans. So much for just dropping by to pick up the photos.

"Good. It's settled, then." Grace pivoted and returned to the kitchen.

Tasha stepped into the snow pants. Philip caught her arm when she wobbled while standing on one leg. She zipped up the snow pants. After discarding her own thin knitted mittens, she slipped the ski gloves on.

Philip put on his own gloves. "Thanks for being such a good sport."

"I don't mind. I think I'm due for a little fun anyway."

Philip peered in at Grace as she chopped vegetables and sang to Shawn, who sat in his high chair. Shawn amused himself by smearing banana on his tray. The aroma of garlic floated into the hallway. A round layer cake with chocolate frosting rested on the counter. His sister had outdone herself.

"Just got to get these carrots cooked." Grace stopped chopping and smiled at them. "You're going to love this meal."

They headed toward the door.

"I wasn't planning on staying for dinner," Tasha protested.

"Well, you make a plan and my sister makes a plan. Guess who wins."

Tasha laughed.

Crisp evening air settled on his cheeks when they stepped outside. Laughter and yelling directed them to a snow hill about a hundred yards behind the house. Moonlight gave the snow a cool blue overtone. They walked past a garden shed, their feet crunching in the snow.

A sled with two people on it swooped down the hill. Mary stood at the top of the hill, cheering. In a spray of snow, the sled came to a stop. Both people, a short one and a tall one, got up and shook the snow off. Travis, the tall one, wiped the snow off his sister's back with his gloved hand.

Philip and Tasha trudged toward the kids.

Philip glanced in her direction. "This will be fun, I promise." Enjoying the moment, he winked at her. "Are you feeling adventurous?"

She lifted her head and placed her hands on her hips. "I used to be able to sled with the best of 'em."

A cry of "Look out below" started at the top of the hill and grew closer. Tasha glanced up the hill as the sled angled straight toward her, but she didn't move.

"Watch out." Philip shouted as he pushed Tasha clear of the sled. They fell into the snow. The landing was soft, like falling in a pile of pillows with a firm mattress underneath.

Tasha laughed. "Thanks for the gallant rescue, Sir Philip."

Philip stood up on his knees and brushed snow off his own legs. "I did the best I could on short notice."

Mary's face, surrounded by a fur-trimmed hood, came into view. "Are you making a snow angel?"

Tasha lifted her head and looked around. "I hadn't thought about it, but since I'm down here I might as well."

Mary plunged into the snow beside her. "I'll make one, too."

Tasha plowed the snow with her arms and legs and Mary laughed. Philip took in a deep breath, filling his lungs with cool, fresh air.

Damaris and Travis grabbed a sled and headed back up the hill. The swishing noise of their snow pants grew fainter.

Philip stood with his hands on his hips, listening to the laughter. The hat he wore had jingle bells on the end that made noise every time he moved his head.

Tasha sat up and pointed at the hat. "Hardly dignified doctor attire."

He loved the warm tone of her voice. "Says the clothing designer who wears bunny slippers. Anyway, everybody has to have some fun."

"All done," said Mary. "Help me up, Daddy."

Philip walked the few feet through the snow and held out his hand for Mary. He turned toward Tasha. "Are you finished, too?"

She nodded, and he held out his other hand to her.

"The secret," said Mary, using the tone of a teacher instructing a class, "is not to get your foot- or hand-prints on the angels. That makes them turn out nice."

"Good advice, Mary," Tasha said as Philip wrapped his hand around hers. "Heave-ho." Philip pulled the girl and the woman up in a single motion. Tasha stood on her feet, her face very close to Philip's. Her lips turned up into a smile. He felt an electric charge that shot down to his toes.

"Thanks for the help," whispered Tasha. Stepping back, she pounded her gloves together to get the snow off them.

Mary jumped up and down, clapping her hands. "The angels are perfect, just perfect."

Still wobbling a bit from the moment that had passed between him and Tasha, Philip turned to look at their handiwork.

"They do look very good, Mary," Tasha said. She squeezed the little girl's shoulder. Mary leaned against her.

Philip stood back, loving the connection that was beginning to be forged between Tasha and his daughter.

Philip leaned over and picked up a sled. "Come on, ladies. Let's go for a run."

They headed up the hill just as Travis and Damaris swept past them, screaming and sending snow flying around their sled.

As Tasha ran up the hill, Mary reached out and

grabbed her hand. Philip felt a tug at his heart. Except for Grace, he hadn't seen Mary express affection for another woman since Heather's death. Philip ran to catch up with them.

At the top of the hill, Philip tossed the sled on the ground and sat on the back.

"Mary, you sit toward the front. Tasha, you sit in the middle."

Mary jumped on the front of the sled and Tasha squeezed in between them, holding on tightly to Mary. Philip stuck his legs straight in front of him so his feet could rest on the steering bar. His arms slipped casually around Tasha's waist.

"I'll push you off, Uncle Phil." Travis had come up behind them, holding the other sled. Damaris was still making her way up the hill, her feet turned sideways like a duck to get better traction.

The sled lurched forward. They skimmed over the snow's glassy trail, made smooth by repeated sled runs. All three of them screamed as they caught air going over a series of bumps. Each time they landed with a hard thud, Tasha laughed. Philip held on to her, enjoying the closeness. The sled picked up speed on the steep downward slant. Air rushed past his arms and neck as he steered them on the smoothest path.

The sled slid past the end of the trail. A temporary wall of snow shot up around them. Snow sprinkled his cheeks and neck. He shivered and laughed at the same time.

They glided to a stop as the ground leveled.

Mary jumped off the sled. Snow covered her from head to foot. Only her brightly colored fleece hat was visible. She swiped flakes away from her eyes. "That

was fun." She shook the rest of the snow off like a dog
getting out of the river. "Let's do it again."

"Like father, like daughter," said Tasha. "You both
have an adventurous streak in you."

"Only if we haven't scared Tasha out of her wits."
Philip touched her shoulder.

"I'm sure I'll recover, but I want the middle spot
again." She brushed snow off Philip's jacket. "I stayed
drier than both of you." He caught her hand momentarily in his own and then let it go. Again, his heart
rate accelerated.

Philip heard a thud as snow exploded around his
back. He looked up the hill to see Damaris gathering a
snowball into her hands and Travis with his arm back,
preparing to lob another one at Philip.

"You want to fight, do ya?" Philip raced up the hill,
leaning to scoop snow in his hand on his way. Damaris
and Travis got off two good shots before he threw his
first snowball, hitting Travis in the back.

Travis shrieked. "I'll get you for that, Uncle Phil."

Tasha grabbed Mary's hand. "We'd better help him
out."

Mary stepped back and screamed, "No way. Kids
against the adults!" Mary shouted up the hill at her
cousins as she ran to them, "Kids against the adults,
guys."

She picked up a pile of snow and tossed it in Tasha's
direction. Tasha stepped aside and bent over to get her
own ammunition. A snowball hit her back. The two
girls giggled as they pelted her several more times before she could fire off her first shot. Another snowball,
thrown by Travis, splattered against her hip.

"Philip, help me. I'm being attacked by munchkins."

Tasha held a hand up by her face to shield herself from an incoming snowball.

Philip stalked up behind Travis and hit him squarely in the back with a snowball.

Ten minutes later, Tasha lay down in the snow by Mary.

Water from a melting snowball thrown at his neck drizzled down Philip's back. He shivered slightly, but still felt warm.

Philip collapsed in the snow beside Tasha. Damaris and Travis followed suit.

Philip gazed at the night sky. A million stars twinkled back at him, one brighter than all the others. The three-quarter moon glowed pure white with only a slight gray marbling.

Mary lay in between Philip and Tasha. The cousins rested not too far from them. The only sound was their heavy breathing.

Tasha tried to catch her breath. "This is why I moved out to the country."

Philip chuckled. "You mean you'd get arrested if you had a snowball fight like that in the city?"

Tasha hit his shoulder playfully. "No, I mean that I never noticed how clear and beautiful the sky was until I moved back to Big Sky country." After pausing for a moment, she laughed. "And I probably would be arrested for being drunk and disorderly if someone saw me lying in the snow staring at the sky in the city."

"This is the same sky Mary and Joseph saw when they were going to Bethlehem." Travis's voice floated on the cool evening air.

No one said anything.

"You're right about that, Travis," Tasha whispered.

Grace's voice sounded faint in the distance. "Time for supper."

Philip pulled himself to his feet and along with everyone else brushed the snow off. The sound of nylon gloves against nylon snowsuits created a sort of rhythm, like a song played only with percussion instruments. The kids bolted ahead with cries of "I'm starving," leaving Tasha and Philip to gather up the sleds.

"Thanks for the snowball fight," Philip commented as they walked side by side. "Most women would have been worried about breaking a nail or getting hat hair."

"No problem there. My nails are all broken off from the work I do. And my hair…well, let's not go there." They trudged through the snow, the sleds dragging behind. Enjoying the moment he had alone with her, Philip was reluctant to return to the house. He slowed his walk.

He stopped and looked right at her. He drew his eyebrows together. "You've got a snowball hanging from your hair."

Her laugh came out in a sputter. "Do I?"

They stood in the glow of the porch light. Removing his glove, he reached up and touched her hair. He looked to the side rather than meeting her gaze. He tugged on her hair gently.

He held up a tiny snowball, turning it in the light. "See there." He gazed directly at her. The brightness of her eyes, the slight upturn of her mouth drew him in.

"You have a soft touch," she whispered.

In that moment, he thought he might kiss her. All these emotions rushed at him like a freight train. He needed to slow things down and sort through his feelings before he did something impulsive. He took a step back. He held his hands up. "Doctor's hands."

She took on a tone of mock seriousness. "And what are my chances of recovery, doctor?"

"If you take it easy and don't get into snowball fights, you have a fifty-fifty chance of having dry hair again."

She put her hand up to her forehead melodramatically. "Oh, Doctor, if only that child hadn't thrown the fatal snowball."

"Uh-oh. Is that soap-opera music I hear? We'd better get inside." Philip tilted his head in the direction of the door, but neither of them moved. She looked at him with an intensity that made his knees wobbly. Her auburn hair framed her face perfectly. He swallowed hard, but could not bring himself to look away from her.

A voice from the door shattered the moment. "We're going to say the blessing without you if you don't hurry up." Damaris stood in the doorway barefoot, crossing her arms and bouncing to fend off the cold.

"Sounds like a threat. We'd better get inside," Tasha said.

Philip followed behind her, still not able to fully process all that had passed between them.

Chapter 8

Tasha was grateful for the interruption because she feared that if they had been alone any longer, he would have kissed her and she would have kissed him back. And that would have made her life way more complicated than it needed to be.

There were a thousand reasons not to fall for Philip. He lived in the city and she didn't. He was still dealing with his wife's death and she had a business to establish; she didn't need the distraction of a romance right now. A thousand reasons.

But still, when she walked into the entryway, she could feel his gaze from behind even without looking. His attentiveness made her dizzy. The sound of children talking and silverware clinking against glass spilled out from the kitchen as Tasha and Philip removed their snow gear. Tasha hung the borrowed snow pants on a hook and almost jumped when Philip put his lips close to her ear.

"I'll give you the photos later, when we can get a moment away from Mary," he whispered, and then held his finger to his lips. He raised his eyebrows in a "keep a secret" signal.

Tasha nodded. Her ear still felt hot where his breath had touched. She was making dolls for his daughter—that was her relationship to him. That was what she told herself all during dinner while she sneaked glances at his handsome profile. He had a straight nose and an easy smile. His light brown hair fell gently around his face with no hint that it had been styled, moussed or gelled in any way. He looked more like a craftsman, like a carpenter or an electrician, than a doctor. In his dress, his demeanor and his looks there was nothing pompous about Philip. He had none of the "I know more than you" arrogance of other doctors she'd met.

After dinner, the family gathered in the living room. Grace held Shawn while Philip and Travis played checkers. Tasha slipped off the couch and sat on the floor beside Mary and Damaris.

"Can I play fashion dolls, too?" Tasha scooted closer to the girls. "I love to dress up dolls."

The two girls were surrounded by piles of doll clothes and a plastic van.

Mary looked over at Damaris as she smoothed a doll's wild hair. "I guess you could play."

Damaris didn't look up as she clipped a pair of mismatched shoes onto a doll. "She can be the dark-haired doll."

"What's her name?" Tasha cupped the doll in her hand and held it close to her face.

"Crown me, Uncle Phil." Travis spoke a little too loudly.

Tasha glanced up as color rose in Philip's cheeks. He'd been paying attention to her instead of the game.

"Oh, sorry." Philip glanced back at the board. "Looks as though you got me beat, Travis."

Both girls stopped their busywork and stared at Tasha. Damaris's jaw dropped slightly. "Her name is Marie."

"Can I put a pretty dress on her?" Tasha asked.

The girls moved a little closer to Tasha.

Damaris picked up a pile of doll clothes and sat them in front of Tasha. Tasha selected a shiny purple dress with gold trim.

Grace looked up from the book she was reading to Shawn. "The girls are just not used to having an adult who remembers how to play with dolls."

Tasha pulled the dress over the doll's torso and smoothed out the skirt of the gown. "Playing with dolls is my favorite thing."

Philip stopped picking up checkers and watched as the girls offered Tasha advice on how to accessorize the dressed doll.

"Here, you can have the pink purse." Damaris handed Tasha an inch-long plastic square with a handle.

"And the gold shoes," Mary added.

Tasha smiled at her captive audience. "That will look nice. You ladies are good at putting outfits together."

Both girls nodded and then looked at each other, passing some secret signal between cousins.

The two girls sat cross-legged with a pile of doll clothes in their laps. Each of them gave Tasha a mystified glance from time to time. Tasha busied herself putting hot pink pants on a doll. Tasha and the two girls took turns holding up their creations and then quickly ripping the dolls' outfits off and trying something new. They giggled.

This evening had been so perfect in such an unexpected way. Tasha realized she had a glimpse of what it would be like to have children and be part of a big family. Mary seemed to trust her more as her affection for the little girl grew. But more than anything, she found herself wishing that she and Philip could have more than just a business relationship.

Philip tossed checkers into a box as he listened to Tasha interacting with the two girls. *What was it about Tasha that was so special?* All the women he had met were either serious career women who had forgotten how to have fun or divorcees who were so desperate to find a "new daddy" for their children or so hurt from the rejection of their divorces they wore their insecurity like gaudy jewelry. Everyone wanted to date the successful doctor. But he had never wanted to ask any of them out a second time.

He wondered if Tasha had felt the same surge of emotion he'd experienced as they'd stood outside, basking in the porch light. Maybe he was just imagining things. Still, it was nice to know he could feel any spark of emotion after being numb for so long.

After the kids had played for some time, they ran into the kitchen to make popcorn.

Philip rose from his chair and tapped Tasha on the shoulder. "Come on, I have something to show you."

Tasha stared at him a moment, then light flickered in her eyes. "Oh, right—that thing."

She rose to her feet, a pile of doll clothes falling off her legs. Philip walked down a hallway and stepped into a room that looked like a combination playroom and office. A computer with stacks of paper and folders piled around it stood in one corner. Behind the printer hung a bulletin board displaying seed packets, invoices and brightly colored pictures of ripe vegetables cut from magazines.

A wooden dollhouse and a box of baby toys occupied one corner of the room. Children's books and gardening magazines stood in stacks all over the floor. The room smelled faintly of apples and old books.

Philip picked up a manila envelope. He felt a reluctance to hand the envelope over. They were just photos he'd copied from ones he had hanging up or in photo albums. But still, they were deeply personal. Each photo held a memory. He probably could have emailed these to her. But that would have meant he wouldn't have gotten to see her. On some subconscious level, he realized that was what he'd wanted all along.

Tasha did not reach for the envelope. She waited, hands at her sides.

He looked away from the envelope and into Tasha's kind eyes. In a way, she looked like one of the dolls she made, the spray of freckles across her face and the curly red hair. She could be a model for Anne of Green Gables. Or if her hair were braided and a shade redder, Pippi Longstocking. She had the wild playfulness of the redheaded orphans in the books he read to Mary.

He pushed the envelope toward her. "I hope these are helpful."

She took the envelope as delicately as she had held Damaris's doll earlier. Her hand brushed the top of the envelope. "I'm sure they will be. I'll treat them with great care."

And he had no doubt that she would. Though he had not voiced his feelings about the photographs, she was sensitive enough to get it. She turned to go, and he followed, closing the door behind him. "They're all filed in the computer, it's just that—"

"I understand what you are saying."

It was the memory of Heather that needed to be treated with care. Tasha had picked up on what he meant without his having to spell it out.

They made their way down the hall. He could hear a DVD playing as the children chattered in the living room. The warm, buttery smell of popcorn made his mouth water.

"You like to go sledding. You like to play with dolls." They turned the corner into the living room. "So what makes you enjoy playing like a child so much, Tasha?"

She turned to look at him, her expression animated. "I don't know. I was very serious as a child. I was an only child in a quiet house. Guess I'm just making up for lost time." She smiled at him. Pulsating Christmas lights reflected in her eyes, making them dance.

"Either that or you are living your life in reverse," said Philip.

She laughed. "It's a good thing either way, don't you think?"

"Kids seem to like it."

"You're kind of a kid yourself. Most doctors play golf. They don't get into snowball fights."

"I hate golf." Shoving his hands in his pockets, he rocked back and forth. He noticed that her eyes had specks of gold mixed with the brown.

"I should get going. I have work to do." She held up the envelope.

"Thank you for doing this for Mary."

She waved her hand. "Hey, it's one of the reasons I started this business." After peeking around the corner at the kids, she slipped into the entryway and hid the envelope under her hat and scarf. "Thanks for a nice evening, Grace," she shouted into the living room.

"No problem," Grace said. "You'll have to come back next week and look at all my fabrics. Sorry we didn't get a chance to get that done."

"I'll do that. Your place is a lot warmer than mine. All I've got is wood heat."

Philip moved up beside her. "I'll be up again around Christmastime. Maybe Gary and I could bring you some wood." What was he doing? He hated chopping wood.

As she headed out the door, Tasha said she would call Grace later in the week. She added, "And I might take you up on that wood offer, Philip."

"Have ax, will chop," Philip joked.

"See you, everyone."

The kids pulled their eyes away from the television long enough to yell, "See ya," in unison.

"Thanks for playing dolls," Mary added.

With a final smile at Philip, Tasha closed the door.

Philip stood at the window, watching as Tasha turned on her headlights and backed out of the driveway.

From the couch where she was sitting with two kids

on her lap, Grace taunted, "I thought you hated cutting wood with Gary, Philip."

Philip craned his neck at Grace. "Don't get started, big sister. You promised."

Grace picked fuzzies off an afghan. "I'm only musing about your newfound love for chopping wood," she teased.

He held up a warning finger. "Grace—"

Grace put up her hands in surrender. "Not saying a word. Not a single word."

He stared out of the window as the red glow of Tasha's taillights grew fainter. After that disappointing period of dating women who were either too cold or too desperate, Philip had vowed that he would remain single and raise Mary alone.

Maybe I should reconsider that vow. Tasha might be open to moving back to Denver.

Her taillights disappeared into the night.

Chapter 9

With only two weeks to go until Christmas, Tasha worked intently on the dolls for Mary, taking time out only to complete the nativity for the Christmas Eve church service. She created molds and poured the heads for both dolls and designed and sewed their clothes. Both the Heather and Mary dolls were dressed in black skirts and red sweaters just like in one of the photographs Philip had given her.

Every time the phone rang, her ears perked up. No one had responded to her ad for studio space. She'd placed an additional ad in the local newspaper—but still no response.

If she was frugal, she had enough money from sales to carry her through February. But after that, her future was uncertain. Every time she reworked her finances in her head or on paper, she breathed the same one-line prayer. *I will trust in You, Lord.* It was easy to say the prayer, but when the bills came in the mail, it was hard to actually do it.

Sometimes when the phone rang, she half hoped it was Philip. Her thoughts had returned to him often since they'd gone sledding.

The final step in making the dolls was painting their faces. This was her favorite stage of doll making because she could really make the personality come out through her brushstrokes.

The doll heads both had a base coat of skin tone when she placed them on a stand and prepared to start on their eyes. In front of her, she set up a bulletin board that had all the pictures laid out. This was the story of a family—a happy family. There were pictures of Heather embracing her daughter, of Philip holding his wife and daughter. Faces smiled at her from sunny days spent on a beach and from ski hills, their poles planted in the snow, faces red from the cold, but always smiling. More than anything, she needed to be respectful of what she saw there. These dolls were for a little girl who missed her mother.

She stood inches from the bulletin board, studying the eyes in each photo. Mary had gray eyes and Heather's were a gray-green.

She mixed her paints several times, trying them out on a piece of paper that had a wash of skin tone on it. After several fresh blendings of color and a constant restudying of the pictures, she felt that she had the right color. Tasha dipped the tip of the brush into the green shade and held it up to the Heather doll. Her hand trembled. The first brushstroke always made her pulse race.

She dabbed the brush on the iris and then stood back to check the color. Satisfied, she continued to paint.

She had just completed the delicate pupils and eye-lashes on the Mary head when a loud banging on the door made her jump. Fortunately, her brush had been pulled back from the doll at the time or Mary would have had a black streak across her cheek.

The pounding at her door continued.

Tasha set her brush down and strode across the floor. As she reached for the knob, the door swung open. A gust of cold air hit her. An elderly man wearing an aviator's cap and a brittle-looking bomber jacket came into view. In one hand, he held a sawhorse and in the other Tasha's computer-generated ad.

He pushed the ad toward her. "Saw this in the hardware store." Wisps of white hair stuck out from the cap. "Wife says I can't do my woodworking in the living room. Biggest mistake we ever made was selling our ranch house with that big workshop and moving into town."

Stunned, Tasha took two steps back and swallowed hard. "I didn't give my address. How did you know to come out here?"

He stepped inside and plunked his sawhorse on the concrete floor. "This is a small community. Everyone knows who Tasha is. She's the artist in the old Filmore barn."

"I keep forgetting that I live in a town of three thousand. Nobody is anonymous."

He leaned against his sawhorse and pointed outside through the open door. "Got the rest of my stuff in the truck."

This was not going at all as Tasha had envisioned.

She had intended to take applications, interview each applicant about his or her work habits. "Well, I—"

"Good, then. I'll get the rest of my equipment." He sauntered out the door, but turned to look at her. "My name's Eli. Eli Smith. Everyone knows me as Eli the wood-carver."

But there hadn't been any opportunity to interview applicants. So far, Eli was the only applicant. Tasha shrugged. "And you already know who I am. I'm the artist in the old Filmore barn."

Eli threw back his head and laughed a hearty laugh that came from his stomach and bubbled out of his throat. His hat fell off, revealing a full head of hair as white as the snow he stood on. "We'll get along fine, Tasha, just fine." He grabbed her hand and shook it so hard her body vibrated.

Tasha wasn't sure about that. She watched as Eli picked up his hat and dusted the snow off it by brushing it against his knee. He seemed very likable, but she didn't know anything about him.

Eli looked at her with steel-blue eyes. "We haven't discussed rent yet. Within reason, price is no object. I need to do my woodworking. It keeps me sane since I sold the ranch."

Then again, she had prayed about this, and she needed to trust God with the tenant He had brought to her door.

Eli strode out to his truck and reached into the cab, pulling out a record player and a pile of albums. As he approached the barn, he said, "Hope you like Benny Goodman and Elvis. I can't work unless I got my music."

She didn't mind either of those kinds of music, but

she thought she might find a way to introduce Eli to the concept of the iPod.

"Can I help you with anything?" Tasha had already slipped into her boots and coat. There was only one way to find out if Eli would work as a tenant—might as well get him moved in.

"Whatever you can lift," Eli said as he surveyed the barn.

Tasha pointed to a far corner of the barn that was on the opposite end of where her work and living space was. "You can set up over there. You'll have to run extension cords. I've only wired one side of the barn." She hoped that he didn't have too many things that required a plug.

"I've got some electrical skills. I can finish the wiring for you."

"That would be wonderful. Of course, I'll pay you for it." How, she didn't know. But it wouldn't be right to expect him to do it for free.

"Don't worry about it." He walked around with his hands on his hips. "You've got lots of space in here." He gave Tasha a hearty slap on the back. "This looks as if it will do just fine."

Tasha and Eli worked twenty minutes hauling sawhorses, power tools, plywood, rough wood, cut wood, boxes of nails, screws and varnishes, and stumps that had been stripped of their bark.

After removing his bomber jacket, Eli placed his hands on his hips and studied the piles of wood and power tools. "Gonna take me a while to get the whole thing reorganized. The missus will be glad to hear I found a place. She was getting tired of finding sawdust in her oatmeal. Do you mind if I build some shelves for my tools?"

Tasha set down a stack of books on woodworking. "No, not at all. The barn could use some more storage space. If the shelves are permanent, I can pay you for materials."

He waved the idea away with his hand. "Don't worry about it." He pulled his wallet out of his back pocket. "Speaking of money. How much do I owe you for rent?"

Tasha cleared her throat. "I thought two hundred a month would be reasonable."

Eli furled his wrinkled forehead. "Reasonable? That's dirt cheap. Let's say two-fifty."

"Ah—okay." Tasha pointed toward her workspace. "Why don't you come over here? I'll need to get your phone number and other information."

Eli followed Tasha, his work boots echoing on the concrete. He leaned on her table and wrote the check. When he was finished, he looked up at the shelves of dolls at various stages of completeness. Beside the shelves was a box full of doll heads, arms and legs. "Looks as if you keep pretty busy. Might want to buy one or two of those for my granddaughters."

"You're welcome to have a look around." Tasha was starting to feel like Christmas was coming a little early. In five short minutes, she had gotten a renter, wiring, shelving and sold some dolls.

His eyes came to rest on the floor where she had set up the nativity she'd made for the Christmas Eve service. "Well, now, that's right pretty." He knelt on the floor.

"Real nice." His hand just barely brushed the sheer,

gold-trimmed fabric that covered the angel. "But you need some animals. Seems like there would have been a cow or two, maybe a sheep there to see the birth of Jesus."

"You're right, but I don't do animals well, just people and the occasional teddy bear, and I don't think there were any teddy bears in that barn."

Eli chuckled. "You're probably right about that. But what do I know? My wife is the one who does Christmas big—always trying to get me to go to those silly church things."

"One thing, Mr. Smith."

"Please, call me Eli. Everybody does."

"Eli, you can come as early as you want to work. I usually get up about five. But I'm not a night person— if you could stay no later than ten, that would be good."

Eli's hands twitched at his sides. "Well, I'm a night person myself. But I can adjust my schedule—I suppose."

Tasha's chest tightened. Eli was very likable and willing to pay rent up front, but none of that would matter if their work styles were incompatible.

Tasha returned to painting the Heather doll's face while Eli organized his workspace. If she could work steadily, she would have the dolls done in a few days. She still had to weave the wigs. She thought about calling Philip to set up how she would get the dolls to him. She was glad to have an excuse to call him.

Tasha found the card Philip had given her and dialed the number. A bright-sounding female voice answered. "Family First Clinic. How may I help you?"

"Is Dr. Philip Strathorn in?"

"He is, but he's with a patient. Can I take a message?"

"My name is Tasha Henderson. I'm making some dolls for his daughter for Christmas."

"Oh, yes. He told me about you," said the woman.

"He did?" Tasha couldn't contain her surprise. Was Philip talking about her to his staff?

The woman seemed a bit put off by Tasha's enthusiasm. After a pause, she spoke in a lower voice. "He just said he was having some very special dolls made."

Tasha squeezed the phone tighter and glared at the ceiling. Now she felt stupid. Of course he was just talking about what she did professionally. "I'm almost done with the dolls. Tell him I need to find a time when I can show them to him. I'll be in Denver at the end of the week."

"I'll make sure he gets the message."

Tasha hung up the phone and paced back and forth in her workspace. Why had she cared whether Philip had told his receptionist about her? The truth was she liked Philip. No matter how hard she tried to talk herself out of it, she was attracted to him. It would be a letdown when the dolls were finished, and she had no more excuses to see or talk to him. You can't drive for twelve hours and then tell someone you just stopped by because you were in the neighborhood.

She opened a bottle of red paint and dabbed it on her mixing palette. She added enough white to produce the shade of pink she desired and prepared to paint the lips on the dolls. Her brush moved over the ridges.

Eli placed a thick piece of hardwood on his sawhorse table. He hunched over a display shelf with a drilling tool in his hands. A coiling line of shavings rose up from the wood. At this distance, Tasha couldn't see exactly what he was doing, but she suspected he was putting scrollwork on the shelf.

Eli kept his record player turned down low, but he had a habit of talking to his wood while he was working. Every once in a while, he would burst out as though he were center stage at the Met, saying things like "Don't you give me no trouble now" or "You look pretty like that" and "You go right here with this little guy."

Every time Eli had a conversation with his project, Tasha jumped. The distraction had slowed her progress on the dolls. Some adjustments were going to have to be made if this space-sharing arrangement was going to work.

The phone rang. Tasha continued to paint. She heard her voice on the message machine and then a male voice said, "This is Philip. Just returning your call—"

Paintbrush in hand, Tasha raced across the floor to pick up the phone, "Philip, hi—"

"Oh, you are there."

"Yes. Listen, I should be done with the dolls by the end of the week. I have to drive into Denver for supplies and to see if some of the dolls I placed in stores have sold." That was a little bit of a stretch. She could get the supplies by mail order and she could just as easily check on the doll sales by phone. "I could bring the dolls by, if you like." The truth was she wanted to see Philip face-to-face again.

"All right, but catch me at the office. I don't want to keep the dolls where Mary might find them."

He gave her directions to his office, and they agreed upon a time to meet.

Before hanging up, he said, "And listen, Tasha. Thank you—for everything."

Tasha set the phone back in the cradle with Philip's last words still playing in her head. When she turned around, Eli loomed over her. Standing about a foot shorter than him gave her a perfect view of his purple-and-brown plaid shirt buttoned to the top. Tasha tilted her head. With the white hair and scruffy beard, Eli had a sort of unkempt Santa quality.

He rubbed his upper arms. "Kind of drafty in this place."

Tasha nodded in agreement. "It's the high ceiling." She looked up. "All the heat rises."

Eli surveyed the rafters. "Need some insulation is what you need." He tugged at his beard. "Yep, losing half your heat through that roof."

"When I get the money, I'll take care of that." *When I get the money. Everything will happen when I get the money.*

For the next few days, Eli came around ten o'clock in the morning and worked through dinner, sometimes taking time off to go have lunch with his wife. More than once, he mentioned that he wished he could work later into the night, but he complied with the hours she'd set. He continued to talk to himself and his wood while he worked. Tasha was still debating whether she should ask him to stop talking, suggest that he leave at the end of the month or just get used to it.

Growing up as an only child had always made it hard for her to adjust to living in close quarters with other people. She and her college roommate had had more than one fight before she realized she was the one who needed to be more flexible. At the time, she had thought that God was dealing with that part of her character to prepare her for marriage and living with another person permanently. What was God trying to bring to her attention this time?

The dolls were completely painted. She put a final glaze on them that didn't require refiring in the kiln. She attached the head and arms to each body and dressed the dolls in their red sweaters. After the wigs were completed, she combed and styled their hair. She left the Heather doll's hair long with gentle curls, just like it was in most of the photographs. She set the Heather doll on the counter and combed through the Mary doll's hair, placing a blue ribbon in the curly strands at one temple.

Tasha placed both dolls on their stands and set them on the counter. She stood back to admire her work. Two beaming faces with eyes that had a human quality looked back at her. She took a step toward them and smoothed Mary's skirt.

"Hey, Eli. Come and see what I did."

Eli set down his handsaw and sauntered over to her workspace. This was one nice thing about having another person around—someone to share in the joy of finishing a project.

Eli walked around the table where Tasha had displayed the dolls. Then he looked at the photos she had on the bulletin board. He scratched his chin. "Those are really good. Look just like the pictures."

"Thank you. I hope Philip, my client, likes them—they're for his daughter."

"You're good at making dolls."

"Thank you, Eli." Why did she need to hear that over and over to believe it was true?

"It's nice to find out what you're good at and then be able to do it, isn't it?"

Tasha put her hands on her hips and stared at the old man with the steel-blue eyes. Eli's comment seemed almost prophetic. "Exactly. That's the way God made us. We're miserable if we're not doing what God designed us to do."

Eli shrugged. "I don't know how God fits into the picture. I just know I ain't happy unless I'm cutting a piece of wood."

"You'll have the place to yourself for a couple of days." While she was sure Eli was honest, she felt a little anxious about letting him work in the studio when she wasn't there. "I have to deliver these dolls and pick up supplies."

The long drive to Denver on icy roads wouldn't be fun, but it would be nice to talk with Philip again and to see his expression when he looked at the dolls for the first time. A romantic relationship was probably unworkable with the distance between them, but she could not deny her growing fondness for him.

It had become really important to her that Philip like the dolls.

Philip hung up the phone and stared at the certifications on the wall. He'd heard the urgency and excitement in Tasha's voice. Ever since that night at Grace's, he had been in a whirlwind of emotions he couldn't sort through.

His nurse knocked on the door. "Candace Dahl is waiting in Exam 2."

"Got it." He rose to his feet and headed down the hall. Tasha was different from all the other women he knew, and he could feel his heart opening up to her. A relationship with her, though, would be impractical. She would have to move back to Denver to make it work at all. And there was something else holding him back that he couldn't pinpoint.

He grabbed Candace's chart off the door and stepped into the room where the nine-year-old girl and her mother waited. Candace sat on the exam table, a look of expectation on her face.

She smiled when she saw Philip. "Hey, Dr. Strathorn."

"Hey, kiddo, how are we doing today?" He studied the blood work on the chart. Candace was a cancer survivor in her eighth month of remission.

"I feel pretty good," said Candace.

Her mother leaned forward, clutching her purse. "She's getting her strength back. Maybe in the summer she can go out for soccer again. Do you think?"

"Your blood work looks good. That might be a possibility if we stay on this path."

Candace grinned. Her eyes reminded Philip of his grandmother's eyes, filled with wisdom. Candace had known more suffering than most people would know their whole lives. Maybe that was what gave her old eyes.

Philip finished the exam and headed back toward his office to record his notes about the appointment. Seeing Candace always brought back his memories of Heather. He was a doctor, but he couldn't save his own wife. The memories of the last days were right beneath the surface. How much time had to pass before they went away?

He sat back down in his office chair and thought

again of Tasha. He knew now why, despite the attraction, he found himself second-guessing his feelings. Caring about Tasha made him feel like he was betraying Heather's memory.

Chapter 10

Tasha had set her alarm for four but woke up on her own at around three-thirty.

Excitement about showing the dolls to Philip made it hard to sleep. She rolled over on her side and clicked off the alarm. It was nice to wake up to quiet instead of an insistent buzz.

When she sat up in bed, chilly air caused her to snuggle back under the comforter. She drew the puffy blanket up to her neck and relished the warmth. After a few minutes, she pulled back the covers. Cold air hit her legs. It would only be a moment's cold while she slipped out of her jammies and into the clothes she had laid out. *The day is full of such promise.* That hope was enough to get her out of bed.

She washed her face, got dressed and drank a hasty cup of coffee. She tossed some protein bars, juice and sugar cookies her mom had brought by in a small cooler. The dolls were boxed and ready to go, and her overnight bag was packed. Yesterday she'd called a friend from her old church who had agreed to put her up for the night.

If the roads were good, she would make it to Denver a little before Philip left his office. She prayed for a clear day with no snowstorms.

Christmas music reverberated from the radio as she drove by farms and little towns. Tasha hummed along to her favorite carol, "O Holy Night." Smiling, she glanced at the doll boxes on the seat beside her. "Jingle Bells" rang out from her speakers and she sang along, loud and uninhibited.

When she crossed the Wyoming border, she noticed more potholes in the road. A light fluffy snow drifted out of the sky, but melted almost as soon as it hit the ground. The patches of ice she encountered were brief. All the blizzard gates were open and the sky remained mostly clear.

Gradually, fields covered in snow and tiny towns gave way to suburbia and larger towns. As she approached Denver, she saw the glass-and-steel towers against a background of mountains. It got dark early this time of year. The sky was already turning gray when she took the off-ramp from I-25.

She found a parking space a few blocks from the high-rise where Philip's practice was. Tasha walked down the street holding the doll boxes. Cars raced by on the street, spraying gray-brown snow. A few weeks before, she'd driven by here, thinking of the man who liked her fuzzy bunny slippers. A lot had happened in those few weeks. Despite her best efforts to deny her feelings, she liked Philip even more than she had when she first met him.

The information guide on the first floor listed four other doctors in Philip's practice. His office was on the fifth floor.

Cradling the doll boxes in her arms, Tasha stepped onto the elevator. As the doors slid shut, she stepped away from the four other people in the elevator. No need to risk having the dolls knocked out of her arms. The door dinged open and she stepped out onto the carpeted floor. She faced a long hallway of offices. Her heart pounded as she read the placards outside each door—Psychological Services, ENT Specialists, Sports Medicine… She stopped in front of the door that read Family First Clinic. Philip Strathorn, MD was second after a Benson Marsh, MD. She shifted the boxes to one arm and wrapped her shaking hand around the doorknob.

In the waiting room, a boy of about nine with a red nose rested his shoulder against his mother while she read a magazine. An older man, with sticklike strands of hair around his bald spot, held the hand of a woman in a wheelchair. The older woman was slumped forward, eyes closed, chin resting on her chest. A woman in the far corner held a bundled baby. She didn't look up from cooing at the baby when Tasha came in.

Tasha spoke to the receptionist seated behind open glass panels. "I'm here to deliver a package to Dr. Strathorn. I'm Tasha Henderson."

"Oh, yes, the doll maker. He's expecting you. If you could wait a few minutes, I'll let him know you're here. He's with his last patient of the day."

Placing her boxes carefully on the coffee table,

Tasha sat in a chair and stared at the Christmas cookies on the cover of the magazine beside her. It wasn't until she put the boxes down that she realized her hands were sweating. She felt like a sophomore waiting for her date on prom night. What was all this nervousness about?

She flipped through several magazines, not really registering what was on each page. The baby in the corner cried. Her mother rocked her back and forth, singing softly to her. The nine-year-old boy coughed and moaned something about being tired of being sick.

Tasha tossed a magazine on the side table and checked her watch. Only five minutes had passed since she sat down. Why did it feel like an eon?

The receptionist stuck her head around the corner. "Ms. Henderson, Dr. Strathorn's in his office. Last door on the right."

Her legs felt rubbery as she picked up the boxes and pushed through the door that led down another long hallway. She passed an empty exam room. Her heart drummed away. That rising sense of anticipation created a tight knot in her stomach.

Her feelings were so tangled. Yes, she liked Philip. She'd admit that much. She was proud of the work she'd done on the dolls, and she wanted Philip to like them as much as she did. Somehow his liking the dolls had become a barometer for whether she should continue the business despite the financial stress. If the dolls really could help Mary with her grief, all the financial struggle would be worth it.

She saw the back of Philip's head. He sat hunched over a pile of papers with a single desk lamp shining on him.

"Philip?" Her voice sounded faint. She cleared her throat. "Philip."

He swung around in his chair. "Tasha. Good to see you again." His smile was welcoming, but there seemed to be something guarded about him. He wore a purple polo shirt and khaki trousers. His white lab coat hung over the back of the chair.

She held up the boxes. "All finished."

"Thank you for bringing them by." Their hands touched briefly as he took the boxes from her and put them on the desk. "You know I could have gotten them when I came up for Christmas. Saved you the drive."

"I wanted to get them to you early—in case you want any changes."

Philip swung back around in his chair. He pointed to the medical journals and pile of papers. "Just trying to get some paperwork done so Mary and I can spend Christmas with Grace. You'll have to come by while we're up there."

"I might do that." She glanced at the doll boxes sitting untouched on his desk. Was he even going to open them? "You need someone to throw snowballs at, huh?"

He chuckled. "No more snowball fights." He held his hands up, palms toward her. "Scout's honor." He stood and walked toward a filing cabinet. "I can give you a credit card payment if you let me know the amount."

Come on, open them, Philip. "I hope Mary likes her gift." Tasha held her hands in front of her and bit the inside of her cheek.

"I'm sure she will." He searched a filing cabinet drawer. "I know I have that order form somewhere." He glanced around the office, hands on his hips. He slid open his desk drawer.

The money mattered less than his opinion of the dolls. "Philip, you might want to open the dolls and have a look."

He threw up his hands. "Oh, yes, yes, of course. I just get bugged when I can't find something." Philip focused his attention on the boxes.

Her mouth went dry, and she swallowed hard as he slowly took the cover off the first box, the Mary doll. Her heart pounded. She couldn't read his expression. The relaxed jaw, the examining eyes.

"It's very nice. It looks just like her."

Tasha wasn't sure what she had been expecting. That he would gush all over her? That he would jump up and down gleefully? That he would proclaim that she was the genius doll maker of the universe?

"Really, Tasha. It's good."

He must have sensed her insecurity.

Without putting the cover back on, he set the Mary doll aside. He pulled the cover off the second doll and set the top to one side. Tasha's back muscles tensed. Her throat constricted. He peered into the box. His face paled. His Adam's apple moved up and down. He gazed at the doll without blinking. His jawline stiffened.

Tasha's heart dropped into her toes. He hated it. He hated the Heather doll. It didn't do her justice. Who did she think she was, trying to make a doll of the woman this man had loved? "Philip, if you're not happy with them, don't feel that you have to pay me."

His trembling hand reached out to touch the face of the doll. He slumped back in the chair. "I hadn't expected…this."

"I'm so sorry. I can fix her. Dress her differently if you like. I can do something else with her hair."

He swung around in the chair so his back was to her. "Please go."

Tasha swallowed hard. She stared at the back of Philip's head as tears welled up. What a fool she'd been, thinking she could ease a child's grief with a stupid doll. Philip saw it, too. He was being polite not to tell her. Why wouldn't he at least look at her? "Philip, are you all right?"

He didn't turn around. "Please go," he said more forcefully.

She bolted out of the room and raced down the hall-way. She ran all the way through the waiting room, down the hall to the elevator. Warm tears rimmed her eyes as her throat constricted. The elevator button blurred when she reached out to push it.

She was grateful that there was no one else in the elevator. Her hands touched the cold metal of the rail-ing as she pressed against the back wall. Quinton and Newburg were right. What kind of an idiot gives up a good-paying job to play with dolls?

Tasha stepped out onto the street. The Denver sky was almost black. Cold wind cut through her, and she buttoned her wool coat to the neck. Wiping the tears from her face, she squared her shoulders and took a deep breath. She pushed through the crowd of people on the sidewalk. Walking would help her think things through. Her feet pounded the sidewalk. Shop windows featured female mannequins dressed in red, green and black velvet, silk and lace. She used to design pretty dresses like these. Maybe she could still get her job back at Newburg Designs.

Philip touched the delicate face of the Heather doll. There was that subtle smile and the piercing eyes, the face that seared his memory. He shivered. Photographs had never had this effect on him. "This was supposed to be for Mary," he whispered. He gathered the doll into his arms, holding it close to his chest. He had turned his back on Tasha because he hadn't wanted her to see he was crying. Stupid male ego.

Philip closed his eyes, feeling the weight of the doll against his heart. He was alone with his grief and his God. A stream of tears flowed down his face. He clicked off the light. He cried for a long time, set the doll back in the box and stared at her. He hadn't let Heather go until this moment. She was gone. That was his reality. He had been holding on to the irrational hope that she would come back. That her death had been some sort of dream that he would awaken from.

He touched the doll's black skirt. With his own light turned off, the Christmas lights and flashing neon outside seemed even brighter. While he cried, he prayed. He hadn't voiced his anger or deep sorrow to God until now. He'd been focused on Mary and what she needed to get past this. Really, his holding on to Heather was probably why Mary couldn't let go.

Did Tasha have any idea of what her talent could do? When he saw her again, he would have to let her know. He'd been rude. His emotional response to the doll had caught him off guard.

He walked down the hall to the waiting room. A receptionist with thick glasses and curly blond hair sat behind the desk.

"Bess, did Tasha say where she was going?"

"She ran out of here pretty fast."

He had no idea how to get hold of her while she was in Denver. He didn't have a cell phone number for her.

He called and left a message on her machine, saying he wanted to get together with her. When he and Mary went to Grace's for Christmas, he would explain why he'd been so abrupt.

Uneasiness stirred inside him. He needed to tell Tasha he had lined up a grant for her to make dolls for the children's hospital and the shelter for abused kids. And he still hadn't paid her.

Maybe when he got up to Pony Junction, he could ask her out to lunch and tell her the good news. Now that it felt like the barrier between them was finally gone, he'd use any excuse he could find to see her again.

Chapter 11

With her hands shoved in the pockets of her long coat, Tasha walked until she found herself downtown on Larimer Street. Larimer Square featured art galleries, craft shops and clothing boutiques. Tasha stood outside the storefront called The Boutique. A window dresser fussed with the mannequins, one of which was dressed in a pink evening gown with silver trim around the heart-shaped neckline. That dress was Tasha's design, but the other mannequins were wearing holiday dresses she did not recognize. Tasha wondered if Newburg really had fired Octavia Monroe, as she'd said she would.

"Come here for old times' sake, did you? I didn't know you were in town. What brings you back?"

Tasha looked up into Quinton's face. As usual, every wavy blond hair on his head was in place. "No I—I've been thinking—" On her walk, she'd stopped by some of the toy shops where she had placed some of her dolls. Not many people were buying her dolls. Just one more confirmation that this doll business had been a huge mistake. "I've been thinking about coming back…to Newburg."

A smile crossed Quinton's face. "Really? I'm sure we could work something out. Sales have been way down since you left."

"Octavia?"

"Octavia is still with us. But Newburg was right when she said you were the better designer."

Tasha stared at the lifeless eyes of a mannequin. "It's not a for-sure thing. I have a lot of thinking to do." She was still reeling from Philip's reaction to the dolls.

Quinton held his arm out for her. "Why don't we talk about it over dinner?"

She hesitated and then wrapped her arm in his. She needed to clear her head, to be alone and pray things through, but she also needed to eat.

Quinton touched her cheek with a gloved hand. "How about we go to one of our old favorite places?"

She drew back slightly. The past hour had been an emotional roller coaster. "This is not a package deal, Quinton. Even if I do come back to Newburg, it doesn't mean we get back together." What was it about Quinton that made her not want to fully give herself to him? She couldn't pinpoint it. It was more than just his lack of support for her dreams.

Quinton waved his hands. "Okay, then let's go to dinner as friends."

"That would be okay," she said.

He took her to a bistro two blocks from Newburg Designs. Tasha unbuttoned her coat as they stepped inside. Sheer lemon-yellow curtains draped to the floor. The countertop, tables and chairs were all silver. The lighting was subdued. A chalkboard boasted such exotic specials as chilled-carrot soup and salmon-mushroom quiche. She'd been to this place a hundred times. But she'd gotten used to the meat-and-potatoes café at Pony Junction. This place felt foreign to her now. Could she return to life in the city?

"I'd like a corner booth," Quinton told the hostess, a college-age woman dressed in a purple satin vest and black pants.

When they were seated, he asked Tasha, "So the doll business isn't what you hoped it would be?"

She bristled at the tone of triumph in his voice. "I'm having a hard time making ends meet, and I'm starting to wonder if this is where God wants me to be." Quinton wasn't the best person to share her disappointment with. Her thoughts turned again to Philip and how supportive he'd been when she'd shared her struggles at the hotel.

The waitress set down two glasses of water and two menus.

Tasha didn't even open the menu. "I'll have the blackened chicken salad, no dressing, just some lemon on the side and some hot tea, something herbal."

Quinton ordered filet mignon, medium rare.

Tasha rested her forehead in her palm. "I can't just shut down the business. I have orders to fill, and now I have a tenant."

Quinton leaned across the table. "How about this? I'll talk to Newburg about you doing a couple dresses for the spring show—set up some sort of freelance contract for you. By then, you should be able to tie up loose ends. We can ease you back into the business."

A tight cord that ran from her stomach through her chest twisted inside her. She could not get the picture of Philip turning his back to her out of her head. "Oh, Quinton, I just don't know." Tears welled up again. "I need to pray about it."

He grabbed her hand. "Isn't it obvious? You were meant to be a clothing designer, Tasha." He winked at her. "It's your gift. It's your calling."

Tasha still wasn't sure. She felt like a boat being washed from the shoreline out to sea and back to the shoreline. What did God want her to do with her talent? She sighed. "I can do one or two dresses for Newburg for now. I could use the extra money."

"That's my girl. Maybe by next season you'll be ready to come back full time." He squeezed her hand. "The new designer isn't half as good as you, Tasha."

"Thanks for the vote of confidence." She wished people felt the same about her dolls. It wouldn't be easy to talk her mom into moving to Denver with her. Maybe she could work out some sort of telecommuting arrangement with Newburg.

When dinner came, they ate and visited, but Tasha's mind kept wandering.

After spending the night with her friend from church, she got up before sunrise, left a note for her friend and drove home. She didn't feel like listening to Christmas music as she drove. Wyoming seemed even flatter and more barren than it had on the way down. At the top of each ridge, she stared out at the lonely, straight road in front of her and sighed deeply.

As she neared Pony Junction, the highway emptied

of traffic. What was she doing living out here in the middle of nowhere? She turned off the interstate and onto a two-lane road. On her way through Pony Junction, she stopped at the hardware store and the bookstore to pull her ads down. She didn't need any more tenants if she was going to close down her business.

It was dark by the time she pulled up to her studio. A chilly, drafty barn was nothing to race home to. She swung the door open, expecting to be hit with bitter cold. Instead, heat blasted her face. She stepped inside. Eli's woodworking shop was set up in his corner. He had made more progress on the animals he was carving, but she still couldn't tell what they were.

She slipped her coat off. She was still warm. Her eyes moved slowly upward. The ceiling had foam sprayed all over it.

Eli had insulated her barn. Bless his heart. Then she noticed the cut logs stacked neatly by the stove. She walked over to the woodstove and tore off a note that was taped on top of the wood. "No charge. My old bones just needed it to be a little warmer in here."

She shook her head and smiled. That Eli.

Tasha looked sadly around at the shelves of dolls. What would she do with all of them if she shut her business down? The thought of going back to Newburg, of giving up her dream, made her heart ache. But what was the point of the dream if it wasn't helping anyone and if she couldn't get her head above water financially?

Her message light on the phone blinked. When she checked the caller ID, she recognized Philip's number. She didn't want to talk to him or even hear his voice. It hurt too much.

All her delusions about the dolls having some higher purpose had been shattered by Philip's reaction. Tasha slumped down into the upholstered chair by the stove. She drew her legs up to her chest and rested her chin on her knee.

The next day, Tasha drove out to her little white church, stopping by the parsonage to get a key from Mindy. She walked up the aisle and over to a corner by the stage where a five-foot-tall poster of Christ on the cross hung. She sat in the hard wooden bench and stared at the poster. *What do I do, God?*

Feet pounded on the carpet as someone came up the aisle. Tasha craned her neck.

A woman holding a piece of paper in one hand and a broom in the other stood in front of her. "I grabbed this off the bulletin board." The woman held the paper still long enough for Tasha to see that it was her ad for tenants. She was maybe forty with straight, stringy hair that just touched her shoulders. Close-set eyes and a tiny ball of a nose gave her the appearance of a squirrel.

"Oh, my ad. I forgot to take that one down."

"I could really use a studio to do my painting in."

"Well, actually, I—"

The woman held out her hand and smiled. Her smile evaporated the dullness of her expression. "You probably don't know me. I'm on the volunteer cleaning crew. I saw you come in."

The woman's words spilled out so fast Tasha didn't have time to interrupt.

"My name is Andrea. I moved here to help my sister. She's a single mom with two kids. Helping take care of two kids is stressful. Painting is my outlet. If I could get out of the house a couple days a week, just to have some time to do something creative, that would give me the strength to help Bridget and the little ones. How much do you charge?"

"Well, I—"

"I've got an income from investments. I used to be in business."

Sales, no doubt, thought Tasha, judging from Andrea's rapid-fire presentation. "My other tenant pays two-fifty a month." Her responses to Andrea were a little slow. She must be tired from the long drive—and from the emotional tilt-a-whirl she'd been on.

"That sounds fair to me. The income from my investments allows me to help my sister without worrying about finances. That's God taking care of us, don't you think?" Again, she did not wait for Tasha's reply. "I'll come by later and we'll make it all official, paperwork, etc." Andrea held out her hand. "It's settled, then."

Tasha rose to her feet. "Yes, I guess. It's just that I—" She was exhausted. Trying to explain the whole complicated dilemma, all the indecision, seemed overwhelming. Tasha shook Andrea's outstretched hand. "Nothing. It's nothing."

"Good. Is there anything else you want to tell me?" Andrea raised her eyebrows, drew her lips into a straight line and waited.

Tasha's mind raced full speed ahead. She had better say something in the few seconds Andrea had allotted. "Do you mind Elvis and Benny Goodman music?"

Andrea laughed. "Not at all. Sounds like fun. I'll bring my stuff by when we do the paperwork. You have no idea how much this means to me. The painting is my therapy, my coping mechanism."

Tasha watched as Andrea strutted up the aisle and disappeared around the corner. She tapped her fingers on the back of the bench, a wild, erratic rhythm. She'd come here hoping to have some peace about her decision to start closing down after Christmas. She prayed through gritted teeth. *God, I'm getting some real mixed messages here. What are You trying to tell me?* Certainly, she wasn't supposed to starve. If business didn't pick up, she'd start incurring more debt. God didn't want her to be foolish about her finances, did He? With some effort, she was able to pray her familiar prayer without clenching her teeth. *I will trust You, Lord.*

Chapter 12

Philip opened the door of the hardware store. Mary and her cousins raced inside. Tasha stood by the checkout counter talking to the owner, Al. Her expression when she saw him confused him. Was that hurt he saw on her face?

Philip brushed the snow off his shoulder. The children all greeted her, then rushed past her toward the toys.

"Hey, guys, we're here to buy a present for your mom and dad," said Philip.

The kids stopped midsprint and stared at Philip.

"I think Mom wants a dollhouse," said Damaris.

Shawn jumped up and down. "Daddy wants a 'mote control car."

Philip shook his head.

"Hey, Philip." Al busted open a roll of quarters by smashing them against the counter. "We got a whole gifts for gardeners section set up at the back of the store."

"You hear that, kids?" Philip pointed. "March over to the garden section and find something for your mom and dad—not for you."

Shoulders slumping, heads down, the kids made their way toward the aisle that held rakes, clay pots and other garden supplies.

Tasha laughed as she watched the children, but she averted her gaze from Philip. She held up the check she had in her hand. "I'll bring more dolls by later, Al."

"Can do, Tasha. We're open until nine for the last-minute shoppers."

She turned to go. Philip caught her arm just above the elbow. "So you've sold some dolls."

She pulled away from him. "Al sold out. It's the first good news I've had in a long time." Her voice was icy.

"I'm so glad I ran into you. Did you get my message? You left the office too quickly. You didn't let me pay you."

"You'll have to excuse me. I have a lot to do." She rushed to the door and ran down the sidewalk.

As he was headed toward the door to race after her, Mary tugged on his sleeve. She held up a little girl's purse. "Will this be a good present for Aunt Grace?"

"No, honey. Go pick out something else." He watched Mary run to the back of the store before rushing out to the street to catch Tasha.

Philip stood on the street as Tasha went by in her van. She'd seemed upset. Why had he talked about the money? That had not been what he'd meant to say at all. She had put countless hours into those dolls. Why was it so hard for him to be vulnerable, to let her know how much healing the dolls had provided already? Why hadn't he just told her that when she'd brought the dolls to his office?

Snowflakes drifted out of the sky. The street bustled with holiday shoppers wearing puffy down coats. Children trudged behind mothers who urged them to hurry up when they stopped to gaze into every window.

He pushed the door open and walked inside. There were other things he wanted to tell her—like how pretty she looked with her hair pulled up in a bun and fastened with gold ribbon. Because of Tasha's doll, he'd been able to really grieve and to finally let go of Heather. He was ready for a new chapter in his life and he hoped that chapter included Tasha.

The children ran up to him holding watering cans, spades and gardener's gloves.

"Will this work, Uncle Philip?" Damaris held up a pair of pink gloves.

"Let's go see what they've got over there, kids." He touched Travis's shoulder.

Damaris pointed to the spout of the watering can. "We could wrap it with a pretty ribbon."

"Yes, a pretty ribbon." Philip stared at the garden supplies until they blurred. The children's voices faded into the background. The truth was his heart had stopped when he came into the store and saw her standing there. Wisps of red curls had escaped her bun and softly framed her face. Her expression was brighter than the Christmas lights. His heart was open to caring about someone in a way that it had never been before.

This wasn't just about the dolls. He had so much more he wanted tell her.

"Daddy—" a pair of garden gloves swatted his arm "—how 'bout these?"

"Hey, Uncle Philip, come back to this planet." Travis jumped up and down, waving his hand in front of Philip's eyes.

"I'm here, guys. I'm here." He grabbed Shawn's hand. He was ready to start dating someone, ready to fall in love again. And he wanted that someone to be Tasha. He had to find a way to say all those things to her.

Tasha dabbed her eyes with a tissue while she sat in her van outside the studio. The pain over Philip's reaction to the dolls was still very raw. Seeing him in the hardware store just brought it all back. She looked at the check that Al had given her. Selling all the dolls was the first positive thing she'd had happen in a while. Still, the news only added to her indecision. Tasha was desperately looking for confirmation for closing her business down, yet everywhere she went, she got the exact opposite message. First Andrea had offered to be a tenant and now this.

She shook her head. Maybe the people who frequented Pony Junction Hardware liked her dolls, but thinking that they could serve an important purpose like healing had been too high-minded. Philip's reaction confirmed that.

She got out of the van and opened the door to her studio. Both Eli and Andrea were working in their respective corners. Eli had several things covered with sheets. Andrea glanced in her direction and then quickly turned the canvas she was painting on. A knowing expression and a little snickering passed between them. What were her tenants up to?

Andrea picked up a canvas painted with a seascape. She dipped her brush and painted over an area that was already filled with color. "Some guy called while you were out, Tasha." The painting looked complete. Why was she pretending to work on it?

"Some guy?" Hopefully not Philip. After she'd made such a fool of herself in the hardware store, she didn't know if she could face him again.

"He said he was from Denver. He's coming up with the contracts, whatever that means."

It was just Quinton. "They're contracts for doing some designing." Andrea and Eli seemed so happy working together. She didn't have the heart to tell them she was closing down the business, not yet anyway.

"The Denver guy said he'd like to spend Christmas Eve with you."

Eli chuckled when Andrea said *Christmas Eve.*

Tasha put her hands on her hips. "All right, guys. What is going on here?"

Again, the two conspirators gave each other that look.

Eli wiped a smile from his face. "Nothing is going on, Tasha. So are you about done with your nativity?"

"Yes, I just need to place the Baby Jesus in the wooden box you made for me," Tasha said.

"Good, good." Eli pounded a nail into a board. "That service should be something else, all the little churches in the community together outside on Christmas Eve."

"You should go, Eli." Andrea smiled as she blotted her brush on a paint-stained cloth. She placed a cap on one of her tubes of paint.

"Naw, my wife's always trying to get me to go to those things." He pounded the nail loud and hard. "I don't know."

Tasha spent the rest of the day putting the finishing touches on the nativity. Quinton was just assuming she would spend Christmas Eve with him. She added a little color to Mary and Joseph's faces and wrapped the Baby Jesus. The faces stared serenely back at her. After he went to the effort to drive up, she'd just have to fit Quinton into her plans. He could come to the church service with her.

Andrea and Eli both left around dinnertime. On their way out the door, Andrea said to Eli, "Now, don't forget about the you-know-what."

"Oh, yes, the you-know-what," said Eli.

Tasha shook her head as the door closed behind them. Those two were definitely up to something.

She took some more dolls by the hardware store just as it was about to close. She called her mom and met her for dinner at the café next door to the hardware store. She needed to talk to her mom about her tentative plans.

The café consisted of four tables lining the wall. The curtains and tablecloths were done in red-checked material. Two old men dressed in ragged coveralls were perched at the counter, sipping coffee. Their cheeks were red from a lifetime spent outdoors. A family with one child in a high chair and little girl of about five sat two tables away, the five-year-old trailing French fries through a pool of ketchup.

When Tasha broached the subject of a possible move, her mom furled her forehead at the suggestion that she move to Denver with Tasha. "If you want to go back to Denver, that's fine. This is my home, and I am staying here."

"You need my help, Mama." Tasha jabbed her fork into the mashed potatoes. "I can't make a living here." Two tenants weren't going to cover all the bills. She dragged the fork through the potatoes, making deep furrows. Why was everything and everyone working against her going back to Newburg Designs?

"I am not moving to any stuffy city. I have lived in Pony Junction for over thirty years."

"They have nice retirement communities there."

Elizabeth shook her head and took a bite of salad. "I like my house. All the memories of your father are there."

Tasha shoved a spoonful of green beans in her mouth. That was it. Mama was not budging. With her salary from Newburg, she could afford to have a home care person come in and help her mother. She chewed furiously. But that was not what she wanted. She wanted to be the one to help her mother. And her mother wouldn't want a stranger in her house anyway. Why did this have to be so hard?

They ate the rest of the meal without speaking of Newburg or Denver. Even while they talked of fabric on sale and quilting, the issue whirled around in Tasha's head.

After dropping her mother off, she drove home. When she pulled into her driveway, a truck she didn't recognize was parked outside her barn. A man dressed in a parka stood in the truck bed tossing logs onto the ground. His hood was pulled over his head, so she couldn't see who it was, but she didn't recognize the coat or the truck.

Tasha slowly got out of her van. "Excuse me?"

The man turned around and pulled back his hood. It was Philip. "I told you I was going to bring you some wood. Merry Christmas a few days early."

She took a step back. Philip's hair looked soft enough to touch. His cheeks were red from the cold, and his eyes held warmth that melted her. Still, she could not shake off the memory of his reaction to the doll, the cold reminder that her work meant nothing. "Thank you."

Over and over, God was providing for her. First Eli had insulated her barn, and now Philip brought her wood. She went back and forth in her mind about returning to Newburg.

Philip jumped out of the truck.

She picked up a log. "I'll help you stack it." Somehow, though, she wished anyone but Philip had brought the wood. She was embarrassed by her behavior in the hardware store. The sooner he left, the better, because no matter what she did, no matter how he had hurt her, she couldn't dismiss her attraction to him. They worked together in silence, stacking the wood beside her barn.

The sky darkened and stars twinkled. Crystal-cold air tingled on Tasha's face. Her knitted mittens got damp, and she slipped them off. She took in a deep breath. The cold was invigorating.

"Did you cut all this wood yourself?"

"I had a little help. Grace's husband, Gary, is back. He gave me a hand."

Tasha picked up a log. It slipped from her fingers. "Ouch." She drew her hand up to her mouth.

"What's wrong?" He came up beside her.

"Sliver."

"Let me have a look. I am a doctor after all." He tore off his gloves. "Your hands are freezing. Why aren't you wearing gloves?"

The heat of his touch radiated though her hand. "The gloves were wet." All those old feelings she had for him prodded at her. She couldn't control her emotions, but she could control her words, her actions. It was like standing on the edge of a cliff trying to decide whether or not to jump.

He turned her hand over in his own. "I can't see anything in this light."

She decided to jump off the cliff. She wasn't going to deny herself time with him…if she could keep the hurt feelings at bay. "We can go inside."

Tasha clicked the light on and walked over to her work area. "I have tweezers here somewhere."

Philip glanced around. "Nice studio."

"Thank you."

Turning on a work light on the counter, she examined her hand. A long sliver was deeply embedded in her palm. She tried unsuccessfully to grab one end of the wood. "It's under the skin."

Philip leaned close to her. "I can help."

"Only if you promise not to nag me about not wearing gloves."

"I promise."

She rested her hands on the table. He flattened her palm by holding her thumb down. "I'll have to cut through some of that skin. Do you have a first-aid kit?"

"Oh, major surgery," Tasha said with a tone of theatrical seriousness.

"Dr. Strathorn is in the house."

How she had missed his sense of fun, joking with

him. She retrieved the first-aid kit from the bathroom and handed it to Philip.

Again, she laid her hand on the counter underneath the light. "Cut away."

He leaned closer to her hand. "This will hurt just a little."

"That's what doctors always say," Tasha said.

She listened to his steady inhaling and exhaling, breathed in the woody scent of his cologne and relished the warmth and tenderness of his hand on hers. Philip cut away the layer of skin with a delicate touch.

She winced only slightly when he pulled the sliver out. He placed a cotton ball over the cut as the blood oozed out, applying pressure with his thumb.

"That wasn't so bad, was it?"

The intensity of his gaze made her heart flutter.

When Tasha looked at him with those wide brown eyes, he felt the same nervousness he used to get in junior high right before he had to give a speech. This was his chance to tell her everything he'd been feeling.

He held her cool, slender fingers in his own hand and struggled to find the words. "I liked the dolls. Please don't think I didn't." He swallowed hard as his throat went dry. There was so much more he wanted to say.

She nodded and leaned closer to him. "You turned your back to me. I thought you didn't like them."

"I still haven't paid you." Ugh, he kicked himself mentally. That was not what he meant to say. Why did he slip into business mode? He wanted to tell her what the dolls had done for him. "You do really nice work—with the dolls." *Shakespeare doesn't have any competition from me.*

Her freckled cheeks turned pink. "I guess I just wanted you to fall all over the dolls, and when you didn't—"

He still held her open palm in his hand.

"And I've lined up a grant for you if you're interested in making dolls and teddy bears for the hospital and the shelter." What was his problem? Why could he only talk to her about professional stuff?

She nodded as though a revelation had come to her. "Philip, thank you. You don't know what a confirmation that is that I'm supposed to keep this business going."

"You mean you were thinking about shutting it down?"

"It's a long story." She pulled her hand from his and drew it up to her collar.

A coldness crept across his own skin where her hand had been. "What you do is important, Tasha." He sounded like such a broken record. She looked at him again, eyes round with expectation. *Come on, Philip, this is your chance.* His throat constricted as his heart hammered in his chest.

She diverted her gaze and studied her army of dolls. "Somewhere deep in my heart, I knew I didn't want to give these guys up."

"Best coworkers in the world, right?" He bit his tongue.

The moment had passed, and he'd traded a joke for telling her how he felt.

"They don't argue with me. And they don't eat anything." They laughed until the laughter faded into a heavy silence that pressed on him like lead.

He sighed deeply. "Well, I suppose I should go."

She held up her hand. "Thanks for the surgery and the firewood—and the confirmation."

He gathered his coat and gloves off the chair where he had thrown them. He wrapped his scarf around his neck in slow motion, not wanting to leave her but not able to say what he felt. He noticed the nativity she had displayed on the counter. "Is that for the Christmas Eve service?"

She took a step toward him. "Yes. You're coming, aren't you?"

"Oh, sure. I'll be there with the whole gang."

Behind the floodgate of this trivial conversation, his emotions welled up. She looked precious standing there holding her hands in front of her. Or was it that she looked like one of those glassy-eyed, clear-skinned dolls that she created? But he could not bring himself to tell her how he felt.

He shoved his gloves on, said goodbye and walked toward the door.

Tasha didn't realize she'd been holding her breath until the door closed. She exhaled and gripped the back of a chair for balance. From the time Philip had pulled his hood off, she had felt as if she was in a whirlwind.

Philip had liked her dolls. She'd been so sensitive, so desperate for his approval of her work that she had misinterpreted the moment when he had first seen the dolls. Why, then, had he turned his back on her? Her breath caught in her throat. Had he been crying? She had mistaken his sorrow over his wife for disappointment with her work.

Tasha pounded the counter with a fist. She'd been self-centered, only concerned about what he thought of her work. She needed to remember that this wasn't about her.

Tasha stared at Eli's work area. There were several bumps covered with sheets. And Andrea had three canvases turned toward the wall. What were those two up to? She was tempted to go over and have a peek, but that wouldn't be right.

She crawled beneath the quilt in her warm barn, feeling very content that night. Philip did like the dolls. She had two tenants to help meet expenses and keep her company, and a grant to help children in hospitals and shelters. She could stay in Pony Junction and take care of her mom. God couldn't be speaking to her any more clearly. This was where she was supposed to be. She rolled over on her side and tucked the quilt around her. Now all she had to do was tell Quinton that when he came to visit.

Philip drove slowly down the two-lane road. The old truck rumbled through the darkness. Once again, he'd forgotten to pay Tasha for her work. It would be an excuse to go back to her place, but she was probably already in bed by now.

His headlights cut through the darkness, forming two overlapping triangles of light. He didn't pass any other cars.

He had blown his chance to tell her how he felt. He would see her again at the Christmas Eve service. After that, he and Mary would be headed back to Denver. He had to tell her then.

He knew now what was so different about Tasha. After Heather died, women had lined up to date him. But the problem was they were seeing "the doctor," Mr. Eligible Bachelor. They weren't seeing him; they weren't seeing his pain. But Tasha was different; she hadn't wanted anything from him. Instead, she had shown a deep understanding of his grief through those dolls. She had come to give instead of take, and that had made him fall in love with her.

Philip turned into the driveway of Grace's home. He killed the engine and opened the door of the truck. A blast of cold air hit him. He thought of Tasha stacking wood with her cold red hands.

The snow crunched beneath him as he trudged up the walkway to the house. A Christmas tree with blinking green and red lights filled the window. It was late. The kids would be in bed by now.

Christmas Eve service would be his last chance to tell Tasha how he felt. If he did, would she be open to moving her business to Denver? He wasn't sure how they would make that work or if she would even say yes to a relationship with him.

Philip opened the door to the quiet house and stepped inside.

Chapter 13

Quinton's arm felt like a chain around Tasha's biceps as they walked from the parking lot to the park where the Christmas Eve service was to be held. She hadn't told him yet about her decision to stay in Pony Junction and make her business work.

He'd shown up at her door around midafternoon, all smiles and charm. She'd put aside the contracts he handed her and suggested they go out for an early dinner before the service.

But now, as she felt the pressure of his arm wrapped around her own, she knew she had to tell him. His demeanor during dinner—touching her face, sitting close to her and casually resting his arm on the back of booth—told her that he assumed that if she was going to work for Newburg, eventually their relationship would return to what it had been. No matter how many times she told him she wasn't interested in him romantically, he simply would not or could not hear her.

As they made their way across the park, the night was still. The dark sky held only gossamer wisps of clouds and a million stars. The air was unusually warm. Tasha liked to think that this was what it was like the night Jesus was born.

Hundreds of people made their way across the snow-covered field toward the open outdoor auditorium. People moved in groups, laughing and chattering as the snow crunched beneath their boots. Mom had to be around here somewhere.

About forty yards from them, she saw Philip walking with Mary, Grace, her husband and their three children. Mary wore the red coat she'd had on when Tasha first saw her at the Denver craft fair. Philip walked holding Mary's hand, eyes straight ahead.

"This is quite a gathering." Quinton patted her gloved hand.

"Yeah, it looks like most of the churches in the area turned out."

"Lotta little towns around here, are there?" She heard disdain in his voice.

"Yes, Quinton, that's all there is—farming communities, towns of three and four thousand."

Quinton shoved his hands in his pockets and rocked back and forth, heel to toe. "Bet you couldn't wait to get out of here when you were growing up."

"Doesn't every teenager think that way? But I got homesick when I was going to college and then living in Denver."

"Homesick for what?" He snorted.

With some effort, Tasha chose to ignore Quinton's

sarcasm. No matter what, she wasn't going to let him ruin her Christmas Eve with snarky remarks about small towns. This holiday was too special. She glanced around the crowd. "Eli and Andrea offered to set up the nativity for me. I hope everything went all right."

The opening bars of "Angels We Have Heard on High" rang out from a loudspeaker.

The stage was built where the rolling hill descended into a valley. A wall of concrete eight feet high and formed into a half circle created ideal acoustics. Gold Christmas lights lined the wall and descended to the floor like glittering curtains. The floor of the stage, a full circle of concrete, contained drums, guitars and a keyboard. In the corner, on an elevated four-by-six-foot platform, stood several objects draped with a sheet.

Tasha pointed to the elevated platform. "That must be where they put the nativity." She spotted Andrea standing by a younger woman with two children. One of the children, a little girl in a purple knit hat, held onto Andrea's hand.

"Nice night, huh?" a man next to Tasha commented.

Tasha looked up to see Eli. "You came," she gushed with joy.

He winked at her. "I have ulterior motives." He caught Andrea's attention and waved at her. Andrea gave him the thumbs-up.

"This is my wife, Gina." Eli touched the shoulder of the petite woman next to him. Gina wore a royal-blue coat that swept to the ground. Her blond hair, parted on the side, was reminiscent of Marilyn Monroe. Only the crow's feet and the lines around her mouth gave away her age. She smiled warmly as she nodded a greeting to Tasha and Quinton. Tasha could picture her in a big kitchen making jam and cookies while ten grandchildren frolicked around her feet.

Tasha's mom emerged from the crowd. She wrapped her arm in Tasha's free arm. "Took me a minute to find you guys. Hi, Quinton."

Pastor Matthew took the stage; Mindy positioned herself behind the keyboard. Several other people Tasha didn't recognize picked up the other instruments. They must be from one of the other churches. The recording of the Christmas carols faded. The pastor welcomed everyone to the service.

Two teenagers standing near the front of the stage stepped forward and lifted the sheet off the nativity.

Tasha gasped. It was her nativity, all right, but it was far better and far more beautiful than she could ever have imagined. Lights had been placed in the straw and hung above the little scene. A cow, a horse and sheep, carved out of wood, gazed at the Christ child along with Mary and Joseph. The background was three canvas panels of a night sky filled with angels whose wings glittered in gold and pure white. The angel doll she had made stood in the foreground.

Andrea turned around and grinned.

Tasha shook her head. "You guys."

Eli squeezed her shoulder. "You know, carving those animals brought back memories of my mama taking me to services so many years ago."

Gina leaned toward Tasha. "I can't thank you enough for giving Eli a place to work. You were an answer to prayer in more ways than one."

Tasha felt a warm glow that started in her feet and traveled all the way to the top of her head. They'd have to do more projects like this. Look what three artists could accomplish when they worked together.

Quinton's voice in her ear made the warm feelings turn to ice. "Looks like the three of you really get along. Too bad it's not going to last much longer."

She clenched her jaw. How arrogant. She had not signed the contracts or agreed to anything. Good old Quinton already assumed he had the sale wrapped up.

Tasha studied the gathering crowd, wondering if she could spot Philip and the others.

Philip and Mary had found a place toward the back of the crowd. The downward slant of the hill allowed everyone to see the stage. He scanned the heads in front of him. He didn't see Tasha.

"The Baby Jesus is beautiful, Daddy." Mary squeezed his hand.

A soft light glowed beneath the manger. "It's breathtaking, isn't it?"

"I wish I could have one of the dolls Tasha makes." Mary drew her lips up into a pout.

Grace raised an eyebrow to Philip as anticipation about Mary opening her gift flooded through him. Would the dolls provide the same catharsis for her as they had for him?

He touched Mary's brown curls. "We'll just have to wait and see, won't we?"

The service proceeded through several Christmas carols. The pastor gave a brief message. The teenagers, this time six of them, picked up boxes of candles and passed them through the crowd. Then they walked around the outside of the throng of people lighting candles with their own. The light gradually worked toward the center as each person helped light the candle of the person next to them.

As the night grew brighter, Mindy sang the plaintive notes of "O Holy Night" with only keyboard accompaniment.

The light on the stage dimmed until nothing but the glow from a hundred little candles provided illumination.

Mindy's song ended. She spoke into the microphone in almost a whisper. "I'd like everyone to close their eyes and thank God for sending His son into a dark world. Just as these candles light up our night, Jesus's birth and sacrifice can provide illumination for our souls."

An unexpected tightness rose up in Philip's chest. This was what is was all about, wasn't it? Light given to a dark world. A black shroud had hung over Christmas Eve services since Heather's death. But now the darkness lifted and Philip basked in the glow of Christ's love. He still felt loss. Grief was not easy and never completely faded. But for the first time, he felt like he would make it.

He stared down at his precious daughter. The candle, held tightly in two hands, illuminated her bright face. There would be sorrow. It would always be present. But he and Mary would make it. The darkness had been self-imposed. He could miss his wife and grieve her loss without being completely ruled by it.

The prayer ended. The lights and music came up. Everyone blew out their candles and sang, "We Wish You a Merry Christmas."

As the crowd dispersed, the pastor spoke from the

stage. "I hope you'll join my wife and me under the pavilion up the hill for hot cocoa, cider and cookies."

Mary squeezed Philip's hand. "Let's go get some cookies."

They headed up the hill for snacks and visiting. Philip scanned the moving crowd. Tasha had to be here somewhere.

Tasha broke away from Quinton. "I want to go give Andrea a hug." She took in a deep breath, glad to be free of the heaviness of his proximity.

About half of the crowd trekked up the hill toward the pavilion while the others made their way toward their cars, probably returning to their homes for private family celebrations.

Tasha found Andrea as she was loading her nephew and niece in a car. She saw Eli and Gina at a distance. She waved and shouted, "Thanks for making Christmas special."

Eli opened Gina's door for her. He shouted back, "Thank you."

She hugged Andrea. "You have no idea how glad I am that you and Eli are in my life."

Andrea pulled back and touched Tasha's cheek with a gloved hand. "You forget. I took a cut in pay and moved from the city, too. You lose something by coming here, but you find so much more, don't you?"

Two voices rang out in unison from the car. "Aunt Andrea, time to go, presents to open."

"So much more." Andrea laughed. "See you after New Year's, Tasha."

Tasha waved goodbye and watched them drive away. She ran back toward the pavilion. So much weight had been lifted off her in the past few days. God had wanted her here in Pony Junction all along. But He'd had to teach her to trust Him with her choices.

She saw Quinton at a distance as she walked back to the pavilion. He stood off by himself, sipping something out of a paper cup. He seemed out of place in his long wool coat. The leather shoes he wore didn't look as if they kept his feet very warm. Everyone else was dressed much more practically in puffy down coats and clunky fur-lined winter boots. Some of the men wore tan coveralls and coats.

She felt pity for him because he was such a mismatch for the Pony Junction crowd. At the same time, introducing him to her friends would be pointless. He would only snub them. He had no desire to get to know these people, her people. That much was clear.

She stepped under the sloped roof of the pavilion. Quinton sauntered toward her. He leaned close to her ear. "Can we go back to your place? I think I've had enough of Hillbilly Hollow for one night."

Tasha bit her tongue and spoke through a clenched jaw, "Just a minute. I want to say hello to a few people." These were the people she cared about. Fine if he didn't want to get to know them, but how dare he insult them.

Quinton put up his hands, palms out. "Sorry."

Grace pushed through the crowd. She wore a red-and-green stocking cap. She grabbed Tasha's elbow. "We'd love to have you come over tomorrow to see Mary open her gift. I haven't discussed it with Philip yet, but I'm sure he'd love for you to be there."

Tasha looked around Grace into the crowd of people huddled by a table that brimmed with cookies and steaming pots. "Where is Philip?"

"Well, he's—" Grace craned her neck and took two steps to one side. "I don't know. He's in there somewhere. Anyway, you put so much into the dolls. We'd love for you to see Mary's face when she opens them."

Damaris squeezed between two adult bodies and rushed out to grab her mother. "Mama, they've got angel cookies with pink-and-gold frosting." She tugged on her mother's sleeve.

"Just a second, Damaris." Inch by inch, the little girl dragged her mother back toward the crowd. "Come over as soon as you can. I don't know if I can hold the kids off from opening gifts, but for sure we'll wait until you are there to give Mary her dolls."

"That sounds good." Tasha saw her own mother huddled in a group of ladies, laughing and complimenting each other on their Christmas attire.

"I'll be there," she shouted to Grace. With a backward glance at Quinton, who still refused to mingle, Tasha pushed through to the cookie table. She picked up a cookie in the shape of a Christmas tree. The sugary sweetness melted over her tongue.

"That was a beautiful nativity." A middle-aged woman with dark hair and almond-shaped eyes stood beside her. She wore a fur-trimmed hat. "I understand you're the doll artist."

"Yes, I am, but I didn't do that nativity alone." Tasha scanned the faces in the crowd. She didn't understand her longing to see Philip, but somehow the evening would feel incomplete without saying hello to him.

"I like your dolls," said the woman. She pulled out a card and placed it in Tasha's hand. "I own an antique store in Flynn about forty miles from here. Some vintage-looking dolls might sell in my shop."

Tasha glanced at the card in her hand and then turned her full attention to the woman in front of her. Here was a market for her dolls that Tasha hadn't even gone looking for. "That sounds wonderful. I'll get in touch with you after Christmas."

This whole time she'd been focusing on big markets like Denver craft shows and getting her dolls into big chain stores. Small-town shows and local markets were where her dolls belonged.

Tasha shook her head in amazement.

Philip only half heard the older gentleman chattering next to him. "We could use another doctor around here."

Faces were hard to identify under all their caps and scarves. Certainly Tasha would have come to see the unveiling of her nativity. His eye caught a flash of red hair. No, that woman with the large nose was definitely not Tasha.

The man cleared his throat.

"I understand the need for doctors in rural areas—" Philip patted the gentleman's back "—but my practice is pretty firmly established in the Denver."

"Well, if you ever change your mind." The man stuffed a molasses cookie with white frosting into his mouth. "The hours are a lot shorter. You get more fishing time."

"I'll keep that in mind...." His attention wandered to the crowd around the table. There she was, standing at the other end of the cookie table. She was wearing a soft pink ski jacket. Her hair fell around her shoulders in those wonderfully wild curls.

Philip's heart hammered in his chest. Tasha was talking with a dark-haired woman in a fur-trimmed hat.

Swallowing hard, he took a step toward her. This was his chance.

A man with wavy blond hair dressed in a long charcoal wool coat came up beside Tasha and whispered in her ear. He put a protective arm over her shoulders.

Philip stopped. His heart fell into his shoes. Was that man Tasha's boyfriend? The man's body language suggested intimacy. He hadn't even considered that possibility. Philip's arms and legs felt heavy, as if he was sinking in quicksand. He'd just assumed she was available.

The blond-haired man guided Tasha away from the pavilion. Several people stepped up to the table, and Tasha disappeared from view.

Philip touched his coat pocket. He had one more reason to see her. Grace could take Mary back to the house and he'd swing by the barn to pay Tasha. That would be the end of any excuses for going to see her. Then he would spend months working very hard to get her out of his mind.

Chapter 14

"Quinton, you're holding my hand too tight." Tasha twisted out of Quinton's grasp. She'd put off telling Quinton about her decision because she didn't want to ruin his Christmas Eve.

"I can't figure out how you could possibly have that much to say to those people."

"That's no reason to yank me out of there." Enough with this procrastination and treading lightly around his feelings. He sure didn't seem to care that he'd spoiled *her* Christmas Eve.

They arrived at Quinton's Lexus. Quinton slid into the driver's seat and turned the key in the ignition while Tasha got into the passenger seat and fumbled with her seat belt.

He patted her leg. "I'll bet you're anxious to get back to the city, back to culture."

A knot of tension started in Tasha's lower back and twisted its way up to her neck. She swallowed hard. "We have culture around here." Why was he assuming so much? She had to tell him about her decision.

"You call that culture, standing outside in the freezing cold?" Quinton snorted. "Didn't you miss the Christmas Eve service at the cathedral, the forty-piece orchestra, the banquet?"

He turned out onto the road.

Tasha stared at Quinton's rigid profile. "Doesn't matter if you are in a mansion or a shack. The important thing is that you are worshipping Jesus." That something that she could never quite put her finger on, the reason why she couldn't commit to Quinton, was becoming clearer. Quinton had all the outward signs of a godly man. He went to church. He had never pushed her for physical intimacy. He knew all the right things to say. But Quinton's faith was all about appearances. And until she had learned to trust God with her future and her money, she had had the same shallow faith. It was easy to trust God when life was good and she got lots of mileage out of her own abilities.

"Of course you can worship Him in a shack." His hands clenched the steering wheel. "All I'm saying is you and I don't fit in here, Tasha."

Over and over, Tasha balled her hand up into a fist and then straightened it out. This was worse than giving a big presentation to prospective buyers, a task she had always dreaded as a designer. Right now, her stomach churned worse than it ever had. Quinton was not going to take the news well. "You don't fit in here, Quinton. But I do."

He laughed in a way that seemed to get caught

halfway up his throat. "What do you mean, Tasha?" Quinton turned down the gravel road that led to Tasha's barn. The soft snowfall had morphed into driving sheets. He flipped the wipers on. The swish-swish rhythm mesmerized Tasha as she filed through the different ways she could tell Quinton she wasn't going back to Denver.

Quinton parked beside the barn and clicked his door open. "Let's go get those contracts signed so I can get back to my hotel room."

Tasha took in a deep breath and pushed the car door open. Snow fell hard and fast. She zipped her coat up to the neck and dug in her pocket for her keys. She ran ahead to open the door. His hand resting on her shoulder as she put the key in the lock was a rock, an oppressive weight that made it hard for her to breathe.

Inside, she flicked on the light and walked to the counter to where she'd left the contracts.

"I have a pen in my pocket," Quinton offered.

Tasha planted her feet. Better get this over with. "I'm not going to sign the contracts, Quinton."

His forehead furrowed. "You mean you want to think about it a little longer?"

"No, I mean I'm not going to sign them, ever." She lifted her hands and swept the expanse of the studio. "This is where God wants me to be. Through good times and bad."

Quinton's cheeks turned red. "What are you talking about?" He tossed his coat off onto a nearby chair and smiled that charming smile. "You can't be serious."

"I am."

He drew his eyebrows together, shook his head and then stared at her. "You don't understand. You were what made Newburg Designs work. We're going to go under if you don't come back."

Tasha felt a twinge of guilt, but she stood her ground. "I didn't realize the business was in that much trouble."

Quinton slumped down into the chair where he'd tossed his coat. "Oh, it's not just you. Newburg made some foolish expansion decisions that really cost us. I advised her against it, but she wouldn't listen. She doesn't understand that she is no Vera Wang or Isaac Mizrahi." Quinton's lip curled back, revealing his perfect white teeth. "We can still make the business work. If you come back."

Sympathy flooded through her. Her words were gentle. "I can't, Quinton."

"You don't understand. I'll lose my job, my car, my house." He slumped over and ran his hands through his hair, resting his elbows on his knees. "Everything I've worked for."

"That may be true, and it may not be. Only God knows. You need to trust Him, Quinton." She stepped toward him. "Sometimes when you have nothing, that's when you see God clearly." She touched his shoulder lightly.

He jerked his head up. "'You need to trust Him, Quinton.'" He raised his voice to falsetto, mocking her.

His anger made her take a step back. "I'm only trying to help."

He jumped out of his chair and leaned toward her. "You can help me by coming back to Newburg."

"The perfect job, the perfect girlfriend, the perfect big church. Is that all that matters to you? Your faith is ankle-deep, Quinton. It's all about appearances. And it will stay that way unless you can trust Him through hard times."

"Just come back to Denver, back to me." He grabbed both of her shoulders with such force it took her breath away. His thumbs dug into her shoulders.

"Quinton, you're hurting me."

His eyes glazed over. "Just come back."

She tried to twist out of his hold. "Have you bothered to ask God why this is happening?"

"I need you." He clamped his hand around her shoulders like a vise.

"Let go!"

He shook her.

"Stop it. Stop it!"

She broke free with such force that she spun sideways. She fell, hitting her head on her worktable.

Stinging pain sliced through her head. She crumpled to the floor. The shelf of dolls above her blurred.

A door burst open and footsteps pounded across the concrete.

Like a curtain descending, everything went black.

Philip could not contain his rage at what he had just seen. Tasha lay crumpled on the floor. He ran to help her up, glaring at the man who had caused her fall, her so-called boyfriend.

"Did you hurt her?" Philip gathered her in his arms.

"She fell." The man spat the words out.

"I think you'd better go," said Philip.

The man pressed his lips together and lifted his chin in defiance.

"Philip." Tasha blinked three times. Her gaze was unfocused. "How did you…get here?"

The man moved across the floor and clasped Tasha's shoulder. "Tasha, are you all right? I didn't mean to—"

"I said, I think you'd better go." Philip's voice was even more forceful. Clearly this guy was bad news.

Footsteps, rapid and rhythmic, pounded across the floor. The door creaked open and closed.

"Tasha, Tasha, look at me." Philip couldn't hide his concern.

She pressed her eyes shut and then open, trying to focus. She touched her stomach. "I feel kind of nauseous."

"You must have hit your head." He touched her forehead gently.

He slipped his arms around her waist and pulled her to feet.

"Whoa." She rocked back on her heels.

He steadied her by bracing her back with his arm. "Let's get you in a chair."

He held her close, guiding her steps. Her soft floral perfume surrounded him. She drifted down into a chair. The mushy old cushions of the easy chair absorbed her. She seemed to relax a little.

She touched her stomach and then her head. "I'm okay. I think I just must have…must have had the wind knocked out of me."

He studied her intently, still not willing to let go of the idea that she had a head injury. "How are you feeling?"

"Kind of dizzy, and I'm having a hard time focusing."

Philip put his face right in front of her. Her pupils weren't dilated. That was a good sign. Still, the other symptoms were a concern.

"Tell me your name and birth date." His forehead creased. He continued to study her, to stare at her like she was a specimen under a microscope.

She laughed. "My name is Tasha. I was born on February 6. Mom said it snowed that day. Really, Philip, I think I'm fine."

"Good. Now grab my fingers and squeeze them tight." He held his hands up, palms toward her, fingers spread.

"What?" she asked.

"Grab my fingers and squeeze them tight." He moved his hand closer to her face.

"My arms feel like I've fallen asleep on them, all tingly and heavy." She wrapped her hands around Philip's fingers. She squeezed tighter. "Oh, I get it. You're doing the doctor thing."

"Right." He touched her cheek with his open palm and stared into the depth of those beautiful eyes.

She wrinkled her nose and pressed her hand over his. "That wasn't a doctor thing. That was more of an 'I like you' thing."

"You caught me." Heat rose up in his cheeks. "That was an 'I like you' touch."

"No, you don't understand, Philip." Her head wobbled on top of her neck as she tried to shake it. "I like you, too, Philip."

He smiled and shook his head. She was still a little dizzy from the accident. "I need you to stick your tongue out," he said.

"What?"

"Stick your tongue out."

"Oh, right. The doctor thing."

His face was only inches from hers, close enough for him to take note of the smile lines around her mouth.

He refocused his attention. "You don't appear to have a serious head injury, but it might show up later." He touched her forehead. She winced. "You do, however, have a nasty cut." Again, he touched her face, this time with both hands. "Sit right here."

He retreated to the bathroom, where he ran some hot water and soaked a washcloth. He returned and placed the warm cloth on her forehead. "I'll dress that cut. You need to be monitored for the next twenty-four hours." He wrapped a blanket around her shoulders. "Why don't you come back to Grace's place with me? You can sleep on the sofa."

"I'm feeling a lot better," she said.

"I won't take no for an answer. If a head injury is going to show up, it will be in the first twenty-four hours. Besides, I don't want to leave you alone here. Your boyfriend might come back." His voice tinged with bitterness.

Tasha's eyes grew wide. "He's not my boyfriend."

A weight lifted off his shoulders. "I'm glad to hear that." For the first time since he'd seen her with that man, he felt like he could take in a deep breath. "Somehow I didn't picture you as the type of girl who would put up with any abuse. It's settled, then. You'll stay the night at Grace's."

"But I—"

"It's settled, then."

She brought her hand up in a weak salute. "Yes, doctor."

He knelt in front of her so she could look at him. "Now that we're done with the medical stuff…and that guy isn't your boyfriend…" He touched her arm in the delicate spot by her elbow.

"I really do like you, Philip." She let out a tiny laugh. "That…that just fell out of my mouth. The accident is making me silly. Normally, I wouldn't be so bold."

He held her hands in his. "I'm glad it just fell out. One of us had to get brave enough to say it."

She leaned toward him. Her lips parted slightly.

He gathered her into his arms and pressed his lips against hers. A rush of warmth flooded through him. His heart hammered in his ears. The softness of her cheek brushed against his face. He kissed her again, relishing how wonderful it felt to hold her. Philip took in a deep breath of her floral perfume and kissed her harder. Her hand fluttered on his neck. Released from the kiss, she gazed at him with brown eyes framed by thick lashes. He touched her soft curls. A dark thought crept up on him. *We can't make this work. I've met the woman of my dreams, but she lives here and I live in the city.*

He pushed the thought away and basked in the warmth and beauty of the moment, hugging her again.

His hands brushed her back. Reluctantly, she pulled free of his hug. "I'll just throw a few things in an overnight bag." She took a moment to gaze at him before heading up to her loft.

He touched her arm. "Are you still dizzy? Do you need help?"

She smiled. "I'm fine. Be right back."

He could hear her opening and closing drawers. She leaned over the railing of the loft and shouted, "Philip, why did you come by anyway?"

He gazed up at her. "I wanted to pay you for the dolls."

She laughed as she descended the stairs and grabbed a toothbrush out of the bathroom. "Of course, the money." After grabbing her phone and stuffing all the items in a small bag, she walked over to him.

He pulled his credit card out of his wallet and placed it in her open palm. "For a job well done."

She swiped his card and handed it back to him. "That officially ends our business relationship."

He gathered her into his arms and swayed back and forth. "I guess I'm out of excuses to come by and see you."

She brushed the hair off his forehead. "You don't need an excuse."

He swayed with her, kissing her hair. What he would give to stay in this beautiful, sweet moment forever.

Then practicality reared its ugly head. Would she be open to moving back to Denver? A business like hers could be set up anywhere. He had a thriving practice in Denver.

Philip pulled out of the hug and looked at her. What was that he saw behind her eyes? The same doubts he had?

Philip slipped back into his coat. Holding hands, they made their way toward the door. "If that guy wasn't your boyfriend, who was he?"

"A former business associate. I gave him some advice he didn't want to hear. Hopefully, it will sink in later—when he's not so angry."

"What kind of advice?" He twisted the doorknob and pulled the door open. The night was completely dark.

"About learning to trust God through hard times."

"I understand," said Philip.

He helped Tasha into the passenger side of his Volkswagen.

When they arrived at the quiet house, Philip retrieved some blankets from a hall closet and helped Tasha pull out the hide-a-bed.

He touched her hair lightly and kissed her forehead. "As a precaution, I'm going to wake you several times during the night and check your responses."

"I feel okay, really."

He touched her lips with his finger "Let me be the doctor here."

"Sorry."

"Good night, Tasha." He heard her soft reply as he made his way down the hallway to the guest room. He struggled with an unsettled feeling as he slipped beneath the covers. Tomorrow would be good. Mary would open her present and Tasha would see how important her work was. But after tomorrow, all he could see was uncertainty about their future together.

Chapter 15

The next morning, tearing paper, laughter and bright lights flashing in her face woke Tasha.

"Airpane. Airpane," Shawn screamed.

A toy airplane streaked by Tasha's face. Not only did the toy have flashing red lights, but it made takeoff noises—searing, earsplitting takeoff noises.

Her head throbbed. Tasha checked her watch—5:00 a.m. Trying to shake off grogginess, she propped herself on an elbow.

"Look what I got. Look what I got." Damaris held up a set of books.

"I hope I get a doll." Mary picked up a package, read the label and discarded it.

Travis sat in the corner, legs crossed, staring at a handheld game. His fingers pressed the controls as he whispered, "Got 'em. Got 'em. Take that."

Tasha yawned. "Are you guys supposed to be up this early?"

"Sorry about that." She heard Grace's voice from the kitchen. "Christmas is the one day we make an exception about waking us up early."

Grace's husband, dressed in a bathrobe and slippers, entered the living room. "Philip told me what happened. I'm glad he brought you over here. Sorry about the early-morning reveille." He held out a hand to her. "I'm Gary, by the way."

Tasha sat up and shook his hand. Gary's buzz cut and perfect posture suggested military service somewhere in the recent past.

While the ruckus beneath the Christmas tree continued, Grace entered the living room with a steaming mug. "Coffee?" She winked at Tasha.

"You read my mind." Tasha wrapped both hands around the warm cup as she took it from Grace. She sipped, savoring the sweet liquid and allowing it to soak into her tongue before swallowing. Coffee in the morning was one of God's blessings.

Shawn giggled as he pushed a skateboard from behind the tree. "This for you, Travis."

Allowing the mug to warm her hands, she inhaled the rich coffee aroma. Gary settled into an easy chair. Grace sat beside him on the arm of the chair. Such a wonderful family. This felt like home.

While the other kids tore open their gifts, Mary carefully unwrapped a box, opened it and pulled out a paint set. "Thank you, Aunt Grace."

Waking up with a big family on Christmas morning was a gift in itself. All her childhood longing for brothers and sisters, for a house full of people and laughter, was fulfilled in this scene. She set her coffee on the little table beside the hide-a-bed and a wave of sorrow swept over her. She planted her feet on the carpet and gazed at the children under the tree. It really was a dream. She and Philip could not maintain a relationship with such distance between them. Sooner or later, they had to face that reality. Visions of them trying to make a long-distance relationship work flashed through her head. Would they drag it out for months, pining for each other over the phone and then fighting because their time together was so short?

Philip, dressed in a plaid bathrobe, entered the room carrying two doll-size boxes wrapped in gold paper and tied with silver ribbons. He gazed at Tasha.

Taking in a deep breath, she looked away. It was so easy to get caught up in the whirlwind of physical attraction. Even now, as the warm feelings blossomed inside her, she knew it couldn't work. Not unless Philip would move here.

"Mary, these are for you." Philip placed the boxes in her open arms. "They're from me." He glanced over at Tasha. "And from Tasha."

"Such pretty wrapping, and ribbons and bows, too," Grace whispered. "You didn't do that yourself, did you, Philip?"

"I had my nurse help, sis. You know wrapping is not my forte." He touched Mary's cheek as she settled on the carpet with the packages in front of her. "And I wanted everything to look pretty for Mary."

Philip sat down on the floor beside his daughter.

The other children stopped their frenzied package ripping and settled down to watch their cousin open her special gift. Mary slowly pulled the ribbon off with her long slender fingers. She tore the tape on each end and in the middle.

Tasha's breath caught in her throat; her heart pounded faster than a drummer at a heavy-metal concert. She resisted the urge to run from the room.

Mary lifted the top of the box off and removed the tissue paper. Her head tilted forward, and she stared into the box.

Tasha could have measured the time that passed with a sundial.

Mary's mouth formed a perfect O. "It's me," she whispered. "It looks just like me."

"Don't keep it to yourself." Travis crawled toward her. "Take it out so everybody can see it."

Cupping the doll in both hands, Mary lifted it out of the box. Tasha could have sworn the entire family gasped in unison.

Grace drew a hand up to her mouth. "Tasha, it's so beautiful."

"What a perfect likeness," Gary commented.

Philip rose to his feet. He stood beside Tasha, touching her back with his open hand. "Yes, yes, it does."

His touch made her melt, but she inched away from him slightly. They both needed to face reality.

"Open the other one." Damaris snuggled up beside Mary and pushed the box toward her. "Go on, open it."

This time Mary tore the paper. The wrapping lay in shreds on the carpet. Tasha felt a tightening in her chest as Mary lifted the top off the box.

Mary's face went white. Her mouth dropped open slightly.

Tasha tugged at the collar of her bathrobe. *Oh, no.*

It's had the exact opposite effect on her that I intended. The doll has made her sad all over again.

Mary bit her lower lip and looked at Tasha.

Damaris peered into the box. "It's your mom."

Mary did not take her eyes off Tasha. Tasha's stomach tightened.

Damaris took the doll out of the box and placed it in Mary's open arms.

Tasha knelt down on the carpet beside Mary. "Her arms bend so she can hold the Mary doll close." Tasha placed the doll with the sweet face and brown curls in the mother's arms. "I designed them that way."

"Look, Mary, look." Damaris rested a supportive hand on Mary's shoulder.

Mary gazed down at the dolls.

"She's holding me." Mary's eyes rimmed with tears. "Mama's holding me."

Philip sat down beside Mary. He wrapped his arm around his daughter. "You can put them on your dresser in your room. So at night when you can't sleep, when you have your bad dreams, you can look up and know that your mother will always love you."

Two steady streams of tears rolled down either side of Mary's face. "She's holding me," Mary whispered. She shook her head. "Mama is holding me."

Damaris stroked her cousin's hair. "She loves you even though she's in heaven with Jesus. She will always love you, Mary."

Placing the dolls on the floor, Mary leaped into her father's lap, wrapped her arms around his neck and sobbed on his chest. Philip closed his eyes and nestled close to his daughter's face.

Grace tilted her head in the direction of the kitchen. "Come on, guys, let's leave these two alone."

Tasha could still hear Mary's gentle sobbing as Grace closed the kitchen door.

Grace gathered Tasha into a big bear hug. Little arms wrapped around her legs. Gary patted her back.

Still holding her in the embrace, Grace spoke into Tasha's ear. "Thank you. That child has not cried, really cried, since her mother's funeral."

Grace pulled back from the hug, but held Tasha's hands in her own. "You don't get past the sorrow until you let yourself feel it." She sighed deeply. "Believe me, I know. I went through the same thing when Mom died. I thought I had to be strong for everyone, but what I really needed to do was cry like a baby. God can't do His healing thing until you admit you are sad… and angry."

Shawn still clung to Tasha's leg. He stared up at her with those apple-red cheeks and fuzzy yellow hair and round eyes as brown as dark chocolate. Tasha swept Shawn into her arms. "You look cute enough to be made into a doll." She kissed his smooth cheek. "I sure like this family."

Grace stroked her youngest son's hair. "I sure wish you could be a more official part of it."

"Grace." Gary poured coffee into his cup. "Let your brother take care of himself."

Grace gave her husband a furled eyebrow/pursed lip look that only makes sense to married people. "I'm just saying—"

"Philip is needed in Denver." Gary stirred sugar into his cup. The metal spoon made *tink, tink* noises against the ceramic cup. "You know that."

A chill like a blast of cold air from an open window seeped into Tasha's skin. She shivered and set Shawn back down on the floor. That was it. All those patients in Denver depended on Philip. What did she expect? That Philip would move here, take a drastic cut in pay and abandon his patients in Denver? She couldn't be that selfish...that unfair.

Tasha leaned back against the counter. She and Philip needed to talk and stop this charade before it went too far. Before she fell totally in love with him.

Chapter 16

Grace's family ate a huge brunch and then settled in the living room to watch a Christmas DVD. The opening credits of *It's a Wonderful Life* hadn't finished when Gary, arms folded across his chest, started snoring.

Grace, as well, looked a bit droopy eyed as she sat on the other end of the couch, resting her chin in her open palm. The children played by the tree with their new toys.

Philip took in a deep breath and tapped Tasha on the shoulder. "How about you and I go for a walk?"

"We probably should."

As he slipped into his coat and boots, his stomach tied into a tight knot. There was no putting this off any longer. The dream had to end. She smiled faintly at him as he held the door open for her. Maybe she had an inkling of what he wanted to talk about.

The snow drifted out of the sky in soft, downy chunks. They walked side by side on a path that led to a grove of pine trees. He took off his glove and held her hand.

"Nice snow," Philip commented.

"Yes, it's beautiful." Tasha's voice sounded far away.

Philip clenched his jaw. Were they reduced to talking about the weather because they could not say what they both knew needed to be said?

Tasha stopped suddenly and tilted her head back. "Ever try to catch snowflakes on your tongue?"

Philip laughed, appreciating a break in the tension. "That's what I love about you. You haven't forgotten how to have fun, how to act like a kid."

"I play with dolls for a living. What do you expect?" She threw her head back again. "Now, come on. Let's see who can catch the most."

"One." Philip laughed but tilted his head, opened his mouth and kept counting. "Two. Three. Four."

"I'm up to five." She bent her head so far back, she wasn't watching where she was going. With a thud, she bumped into Philip. "Oh, sorry."

Philip touched her upper arm. His face was only inches from hers, his gaze unwavering. "We can't play like children forever." His voice was low, almost a whisper.

She gazed at him with those bright, beautiful eyes. "I know. I've gone over a thousand scenarios to try to make this thing work. I can't afford to have a business anywhere near Denver. Mom is not going to leave Pony

Junction. I need to be close to her. You can't leave the city. People depend on you."

He leaned close to her and touched her hair. "I've gone over it in my head, too. I don't want you to give up your business. You would resent me for taking your dream away. What you do is important."

"Just my luck. I finally meet a guy who respects my work and he may as well be living on Mars." Her eyes glazed. "Let's just walk together one last time." She held out her hand to him. "I like you more than I can say."

"Me, too." He wrapped his hand around hers.

Dried branches crushed beneath their feet as they entered an evergreen grove.

"One of the other doctors is going on a missionary trip. I'll be picking up his patient load."

Tasha closed her eyes. "That means even less time for you to come visit Grace and the gang."

"I'll have time off at Easter," he said.

They were both having a hard time letting the idea of being a couple go. "Let's not torture each other. We can't make this work. We'll only end up hating each other."

"Sometimes I wish you weren't so wise, Tasha."

They trudged forward, both of them staring at the ground. The heavy canopy of trees did not allow much light in. Tasha shivered as the temperature dropped. She squeezed Philip's hand even tighter.

"Tasha, there is something I want you to know. Something you need to know." He stopped, shifting his weight from foot to foot. "This isn't easy for me."

"Go ahead." Her expression was open, without judgment.

He kicked the snow with his boot. "The way Mary reacted when she saw those dolls…" He glanced at her and then looked upward. "That's the same way I reacted. Grief is such a private thing." He looked right at her. "Your dolls do offer healing."

"Thanks," she said.

"You've done more for Mary and me than anyone," he whispered. "Thank you for understanding our sorrow."

Tasha melted into his embrace. As he held her, he found himself wishing the moment could go on forever.

The citrus scent of Tasha's hair enveloped Philip. He closed his eyes. Everything she had said was true. God was sending them in opposite directions, and they would only end up hating each other if they pretended it wasn't true.

He drew her closer, reluctant for the hug to end. He listened to their steady breathing and the rush of wind that creaked through the top of the trees.

With his gloved hand he touched her hair, her temple, her cheek. She drew back from the hug and gazed at him. He pulled his glove off and touched her cheek. He kissed her gently on the lips and then on her forehead. He would lock away this moment forever. Every time he smelled citrus or saw a redhead, he would be reminded of her. He kissed her again.

Slowly she eased herself from the kiss and then from the hug. "We should get back to the house, Philip."

"Yes, the wind is picking up a bit."

"Don't tell me we are reduced to talking about the weather again." She stepped in front of him and moved toward the house.

He laughed, but offered no other comment.

"I'll ask Grace to drive me back to my place. So we don't have to try to come up with small talk."

He memorized the way her curly red hair draped over the soft pink fabric of her coat. The way she would take small careful steps over the icy patches on the trail and then return to that easy, confident stride. Here was a woman who knew who she was and where God wanted her to be. She didn't need a man to affirm her. That was what made her so attractive—and so out of reach.

He watched her enter the house. She offered him a faint smile and a wave before going inside. The door closed behind her with a shattering echo.

He stood for a long time with the chill wind stinging his skin and the snow jabbing him with icy needles. He listened to his own breathing. He clapped his gloves together to shake off the snow.

Not wanting to go into the house and see her again, he trudged to the back of the house, picked up a log from the woodpile and placed it on the chopping block. He raised the ax and swung it down on the piece of wood with an earsplitting intensity.

By the time Grace's car roared to life and pulled out of the driveway, he was breathing heavily and surrounded by a pile of split logs. He slammed another log onto the chopping block.

Out of his peripheral vision, he saw Grace's car as it eased out onto the main road. He raised the ax, took a deep breath and dropped the ax on the log. The log, rotten on the inside, split into a thousand pieces.

Philip could see his breath as he exhaled. The ache inside, like a vise clamping over his heart, made it even harder to breathe.

He listened for a long time, his face tingling from the cold, until the rumble of the car's engine faded into the distance.

Chapter 17

Leaves budded on the trees as Tasha drove toward Pony Junction. The sky was robin's-egg blue with big puffy clouds. This was why God made winter—so you could appreciate spring.

She glanced over at the pile of dolls she'd boxed and stacked in the passenger seat. She was one of the featured artists at Pony Junction's tenth annual spring craft fair. Not exactly the craft fair at the Four Winds Hotel, but not as stressful, either. Business had picked up since Christmas. Her customers were at little craft fairs and in the grocery stores that also served as post offices and gas stations in the rural parts of the Northwest. She'd also found her niche selling dolls on the internet.

Tasha rolled her window down and took in a deep breath of fresh air as she turned into a parking lot by

Main.Street. The whole downtown area had been sectioned off so vendors could set up on the street and the sidewalk. She pushed open her door, hopped down and raced to the back of her van.

"Let me give you a hand with those." Eli came up beside her.

"Never refuse free help, I always say." Tasha opened her van doors, pulled out more dolls and placed them in Eli's arms.

The old man laughed, and they made their way past the booths to where Tasha was set up. Andrea and Eli had their booths on either side of Tasha's. Andrea had worked all winter painting soft watercolor landscapes, fields of flowers and children playing. Eli had an assortment of carved animals and people, ornate wooden shelves and children's toys in his booth.

Tasha carefully placed each doll on a shelf and then checked her watch. She still had half an hour before the bell rang and the shoppers were officially allowed in. Of course, all the crafters had already been around to each other's booths to buy things. Tasha smiled. Would the shoppers wonder why there were sold signs on so many items even before the booths were open?

Tasha took out the mail she'd grabbed on her way to the show and rifled through it. Across the street, several workers carrying boards and wearing yellow hard hats filled the door of the Pony Junction Hotel, a two-story brick structure built around the turn of the past century.

"What's going on over there?" Tasha tossed the junk mail on the counter.

Eli placed a carved duck on his display table beside

a child's wooden airplane. "I guess some hotshot from out of town is remodeling to put an office in there. He's taking up the whole third floor."

"Anyone we know?" She stared down at an envelope with an unfamiliar address.

"I haven't heard one way or the other." Crossing his legs at the ankle, Eli settled into the rocking chair he always brought with him. He pulled a piece of wood out of one pocket and a knife out of another. He whittled while they visited.

Tasha stared at the envelope. The address was from a place in Oregon. The handwriting, with the printed letters evenly spaced, looked vaguely familiar. She ripped open the letter and unfolded it. Quinton's signature was at the bottom.

Tasha,
I'm writing this letter to thank you. You said my faith was only ankle-deep.

And you were right. Newburg kept making one bad business decision after another.

She insisted on the expansions. Newburg Designs went under. The last time I saw her she was muttering something about going back to Idaho and opening a quilt shop. I lost everything—and then I learned to trust God.

You won't believe what I am doing. I am a counselor at a camp for at-risk boys. I came out here for a job interview with an ad agency. I didn't get that job, but I saw an ad in the paper for this one. I was desperate for money, and I thought, "How hard could it be?" We teach these

boys how to hike, rock climb and kayak, and
somewhere in there we tell them about Jesus. I
even get my clothes dirty once in a while. Thank
you for the courage to speak the truth to me. It
took a long time for it to sink in.

I've met a wonderful woman who manages
the kitchen at the camp.

All of this wouldn't have happened if I'd clung
to my old life.
Thank you,
Quinton

Warmth spread through Tasha. She folded the letter
and put it away in her cash box. That was one worth
keeping. Taking in a breath of fresh air, she closed
her eyes and basked in the heat of the sun on her face.

The shoppers had begun to gather at the ropes on
either end of Main Street. The big clock above the bank
chimed nine times. Craft fair organizers unhooked the
ropes. Like chicks scampering toward pieces of cracked
corn, people flooded into the fair, snatching up items
at the booths.

"Oh, my, this is just adorable." A woman with
plastic-rimmed glasses and hair a shade of red that
occurred nowhere in the natural world held up one of
Tasha's fairy dolls. The woman touched the transparent wings attached to the doll's back.

"She is pretty, isn't she?" The doll stood about ten
inches high and wore a short circle skirt made of shim-
mering fabric. It had taken Tasha several tries to paint
the mischievous look on the doll's porcelain face. Once
she'd perfected the arched eyebrows, almond-shaped

eyes and pursed lips, she was able to create a whole series of them.

"I collect fairies." The woman readjusted the enormous purse she had slung over her shoulder. She held the doll up and rotated it in her hand. "How many of them do you have?" She set the doll back on the shelf.

"I did a collection of fifteen."

The woman clapped her hands. "I'll take five."

While Tasha boxed up the dolls, the woman browsed through Tasha's booth.

"Now, this—" the woman pointed to a doctor doll in a white coat "—looks like something out of a Norman Rockwell painting." The doctor was bent over a patient, a little boy, encouraging him to open his mouth wide through demonstration. A teddy bear was tucked in the little boy's arm. "I see you've called him Dr. Phil. That's funny. Not the Dr. Phil from the television. Wherever did you get such an idea?"

"Just out of my own head." Tasha placed the last top on the fifth box. *Out of my own lovesick head.* If she could use the dolls for therapy for other people, she could do the same for herself. The treatment had been only partially effective, though. Dr. Phil was a hard man to forget.

"Can I leave these here until I'm done shopping?"

"Sure. I'll set them under the counter and put your name on them."

The woman wandered over to Andrea's booth. "Do you have any paintings of fairies?"

This lady was going to need a shopping cart. Tasha's fairies had inspired both Andrea and Eli. Tasha glanced over at Eli, who was pulling the carved fairies from a back shelf and placing them front and center. He winked at Tasha.

Andrea laid four fairy paintings out for the woman to look at. The woman's hands fluttered up to her mouth and she emitted an audible gasp.

Tasha tried to picture what a house full of fairies looked like: fairy wallpaper, fairy salt and pepper shakers, a toaster cover made out of fairy fabric. She listened to the woman's oohs and aahs over Andrea's paintings.

Tasha went through the rest of her mail. She opened her bank statement. She sure wasn't getting rich, but at least most of her debt was paid off.

"Long time, no see, stranger."

Tasha looked up into Grace's bright face.

"Grace." Tasha gave her a hug. "I'm sorry I didn't come by. I was just afraid I would run into—"

"I understand. So how are things for you? We are knee-deep in the dirt trying to get things planted." Grace held up her hands, revealing dirty fingernails. "I needed a breather. I was seeing seed packets in my sleep. Gary's watching the kids, so I can shop by myself."

"Thanks for stopping by."

Grace grinned. The smile took up most of her face, and there was a glint in her eyes. "I know something you don't know."

"What?"

"I'm not telling. It's a secret."

"Grace, have you been taking lessons from your kids?"

She twisted her fingers over her lips as though she were locking them. "I'm not telling."

"Come on. What is it? You found a cheap fabric supplier?"

"No. Better than that."

"You know of a millionaire who wants to buy all my dolls?"

Grace shook her head. "You'll figure it out."

Tasha sighed dramatically. "Whatever."

Grace walked across the street to a quilting booth.

By noon, the crowd thinned a bit. Eli and Andrea brought their chairs and sack lunches over to Tasha's booth.

"We should have done more fairies." Eli munched on a ham sandwich.

"You never know how the market is going to shift." Andrea popped a grape into her mouth.

"One day roosters and cows are the in thing, and the next thing you know fairies are all the rage," Tasha joked, and bit into a chocolate-chip cookie her mother had made.

Eli looked out at the crowd. "You can't follow trends just to make money. Got to do what you love."

"That's truer than you know, Eli." A tone of seriousness entered Tasha's voice.

Eli offered Tasha a grandfatherly smile and patted her back.

After lunch, the crowd increased. As she closed up her lunch box, she had the odd feeling that someone was staring at her. She opened her eyes and gazed out into the crowd.

The people in front of her milled around, none of

them looking her way. Slowly the crowd dispersed. She noticed his tennis shoes first. Her eyes wandered up from the jeans to the button-down red-plaid shirt, to the brown hair. And then she gazed into his rich brown eyes.

"Philip," she whispered.

He strode toward her, and her heartbeat quickened. Like warm ripples of electricity, she felt a wild excitement when he smiled. An excitement she'd managed to keep at bay for months. She was fine. She could keep it under control as long as she didn't see him. Her jaw tightened as her hand balled into a fist. And now he'd come back to torture her—to remind her of how much she cared about him and how impractical a relationship would be.

She pointed a finger at him. "Don't come one step closer."

Philip planted his feet. "What?"

"I don't care how gorgeous you are. I'm not going to be your part-time girlfriend, available to you for holidays and vacations and left behind when you just fly off to the big city. I thought we had an understanding."

He grinned. "You think I'm gorgeous."

"Philip, you're not hearing me. Don't tease me with your presence. It's not nice."

His cheeks grew red. "You think I'm gorgeous."

"Yes, and kind and gentle and intelligent, but none of that matters."

He took a step toward her.

She took a step back. "I said stop it. This is nervy, Philip."

He glanced sideways and gazed at her Dr. Phil doll.

Her cheeks warmed as she gathered the doll up and placed it on the counter behind her. "I needed to get over you somehow." A tangle of conflicting emotions wrestled inside her. She wanted to fall into his arms, to be close to him. At the same time, she felt a tightening in her stomach, a rising anger. How could he be this cruel? What could he offer her—an afternoon together?

He gathered her into his arms so quickly, she didn't have time to resist. He spun her around one hundred and eighty degrees and pointed to the old hotel where the construction workers were.

"You see that building over there? That is where Dr. Phil will be telling all the neighborhood children to open wide."

Hope fluttered through Tasha like a million butterflies. "But your practice in Denver…?" Could what he was saying really be true?

"The missionary trip fell through for the other doctor. It made me realize that taking on other people's workloads was my final coping mechanism for my grief. I needed to stop burying myself in my job. I wasn't spending enough time with Mary. And—" he drew her closer "—I was too far away from the woman I love."

"Oh, Philip," Tasha gushed. She wrapped her arms around his neck and he swung her around.

"It's less money. But I'll have more time with Mary and with you." He kissed her. "I hear the fishing's not bad around here."

She traced the outline of his lips with her finger. "The sledding is pretty good, too."

"And I hear the snowball fights are something else."

She gazed adoringly at her life-size Dr. Phil as he held her. The prospect of spending winters and springs and summers with Philip and Mary stretched out before her. She looked forward to many more Christmases together. The season would always be a reminder of how her wish had been granted so abundantly that Christmas.

* * * * *

REQUEST YOUR FREE BOOKS!

2 FREE INSPIRATIONAL NOVELS
PLUS 2
FREE
MYSTERY GIFTS

Love Inspired

LIDIR13R

REQUEST YOUR FREE BOOKS!

2 FREE INSPIRATIONAL NOVELS
PLUS 2
FREE
MYSTERY GIFTS

Love Inspired
HISTORICAL
INSPIRATIONAL HISTORICAL ROMANCE

YES! Please send me 2 FREE Love Inspired® Historical novels and my 2 FREE mystery gifts (gifts are worth about $10). After receiving them, if I don't wish to receive any more books, I can return the shipping statement marked "cancel." If I don't cancel, I will receive 4 brand-new novels every month and be billed just $4.74 per book in the U.S. or $5.24 per book in Canada. That's a savings of at least 21% off the cover price. It's quite a bargain! Shipping and handling is just 50¢ per book in the U.S. and 75¢ per book in Canada.* I understand that accepting the 2 free books and gifts places me under no obligation to buy anything. I can always return a shipment and cancel at any time. Even if I never buy another book, the two free books and gifts are mine to keep forever.

102/302 IDN F5CY

Name	(PLEASE PRINT)	
Address		Apt. #
City	State/Prov.	Zip/Postal Code

Signature (if under 18, a parent or guardian must sign)

Mail to the Harlequin® Reader Service:
IN U.S.A.: P.O. Box 1867, Buffalo, NY 14240-1867
IN CANADA: P.O. Box 609, Fort Erie, Ontario L2A 5X3

Want to try two free books from another series?
Call 1-800-873-8635 or visit www.ReaderService.com.

* Terms and prices subject to change without notice. Prices do not include applicable taxes. Sales tax applicable in N.Y. Canadian residents will be charged applicable taxes. Offer not valid in Quebec. This offer is limited to one order per household. Not valid for current subscribers to Love Inspired Historical books. All orders subject to credit approval. Credit or debit balances in a customer's account(s) may be offset by any other outstanding balance owed by or to the customer. Please allow 4 to 6 weeks for delivery. Offer available while quantities last.

Your Privacy—The Harlequin® Reader Service is committed to protecting your privacy. Our Privacy Policy is available online at www.ReaderService.com or upon request from the Harlequin Reader Service.

We make a portion of our mailing list available to reputable third parties that offer products we believe may interest you. If you prefer that we not exchange your name with third parties, or if you wish to clarify or modify your communication preferences, please visit us at www.ReaderService.com/consumerschoice or write to us at Harlequin Reader Service Preference Service, P.O. Box 9062, Buffalo, NY 14269. Include your complete name and address.

LIHDIR13R

Reader Service.com

Manage your account online!

- Review your order history
- Manage your payments
- Update your address

---

*We've designed
the Harlequin® Reader Service
website just for you.*

Enjoy all the features!

- Reader excerpts from any series
- Respond to mailings and
  special monthly offers
- Discover new series available to you
- Browse the Bonus Bucks catalog
- Share your feedback

Visit us at:
ReaderService.com